MPM

MPope Media

Lincoln's Ghetto
The America
Many Call Home

Michael R. Pope

Lincoln's Ghetto Series

LINCOLN'S WAR

BOOK - 4

MPM
MPope Media

To
THE CREATOR
MY SPIRIT IS IN YOUR HANDS

Book 4
Lincoln's War

THE WIND

"Those who deny freedom to others deserve it not for themselves and under a just God, cannot retain it."

Abraham Lincoln

RE-CAP OF BOOK 3 - LINCOLN'S SHAME

The tale took a nasty turn as an improbable series of violent dominoes began to fall caused by a local young criminal.

The two Mob imbeciles took in a juvenile delinquent trying to keep him quiet and not bring unwanted attention to their presence in Lincoln. But their idiotic intent turned the town upside down, jeopardizing the entire conspiracy.

In Chicago, Percy called in a sultry and savvy Chicago journalist to use some shady tactics to draw out the story about Darnell on the ground under the cover of legitimate work for Chicago TV news.

As bodies fell, Darnell attended more local events learning more about the people, and creepy behaviors in town. Chuck and Liz attempted but failed to enlighten him about his pending inheritance.

The Deacon stumbled his heathen ways into more information about the untimely adoption of Darnell. The South Side crew's activities spun up with greater urgency as more information leaked out.

A hidden Hebrew sect living in the shadows of town emerged by way of the Chicago African Israelites bringing added value to Percy's quest to find more answers.

The mob's presence began to implode as the juvenile delinquent created more problems for them.

The entire McDougle conspiracy to attain the spoils of Abe Lincoln's will began fall into jeopardy. The series of events sent McDougle on a war path having to course correct before the Vatican forces arrived to clean house.

The Mob boss began to feel increasing pressure from the Vatican to fix the mess or get fixed.

Everything changed as Percy and his team came out of the shadows to defend the unthinkable, the murder charge against his son Darnell.

With the operation for land and power now at risk, both sides scrambled to re-set and face off.

"The elixir is so devilishly relish that they would sacrifice a lamb to get it."

Contents

Book 4 - LINCOLN'S WAR

Extras

Song List

Photo Album

All Books in the Series

Links to Lincoln's Ghetto

Connect with the Author

Part 1

RESET

"Don't worry when you are not recognized,
but strive to be worthy of recognition."
Abraham Lincoln
$2,000,000 and above
$100,000 - $249,999
Magnetrol International

"Everybody listen, you may not agree
But all of ya'll should try it one time
And maybe you'll see
Well I know it ain't easy, and when it won't happen over night
But Lord if you just touch one person you're doing alright
Love can move all the world
Love can cure
Everyone who hears and adheres
Love contained
Can't be loved too great for it can't manifest itself
People wake up because save the world from within
Want this feeling, feeling within
Let some words to be expressed myself
What the funk, we can really save
Because it constantly changes
People wake up and go change the world from within"

George Duke - LOVE - 1974

CHAPTER 1

COMIC RELIEF

Goode, Pope and Associates. How may I direct your call?"

"Tony Pope, please."

"Who may I say is calling?"

"Captain Marvel."

"Uh, ok. One moment please."

"What's up Dez?" Tony Pope answered with a smirk.

"Ok, you didn't tell me this was going to be about fucked up murder and shit! I DON'T DO FUCKING MURDER BRO!" Dez held the phone closer to his mouth.

"Calm the down will ya! This shit gone off the rails and…."

"Off the rails! Off the rails bro?! I came down here to get away from all that craziness. We don't do murders and gangs and dope and shit down here. What the fuck you got me into now?! I don't want to blow a good thing. I mean what man!? WHAT!"

"Look. I need you to keep your head on straight. Nobody knows you have any skin in this, ok? I need you to go to the jail and talk to him. Find out what you can, how this happened. He trusts you. Just be real with him. This ain't Wakanda Dez. This is reality. Time to live in it. He's a good kid. This makes no sense. Talk to him. We need you…no, he needs you. He needs someone to trust right now. Don't wait!"

"Damnit! Ok. I'll go see him. But you gotta stop putting me in the middle of your shit!"

"Bring him some books, good ones. Falcon, Panther, Luke, hell I don't know, Playboy or Club. Whatever you guys be lookin at. Anything but Captain. Just get him talking okay?"

"Ugghhh. Okay! Damnit! Yea I got him. He is something else. One of a kind."

"I know Dez. I know."

"How does this happen? What the hell is going on down here? Ever since he came here the place done flipped."

"Understand. There's other stuff going on because he's there."

"What do you mean?"

"We are investigating the Mob being on this."

"THE MOB!"

"Seems they have an interest in Darnell also."

"Darnell? Why?"

"Yup. Why? We are connecting some leads right now. I'm working with Butch."

"Oh my God! Not Butch! That means this place'll be crawlin with feds. Butch will turn this place upside down and leave a pile of shit in his wake. You know how tuned up he gets when he sinks his hooks into these things. Remember the fight at the church? Became a fucking Vietnam!"

"Yep, went from an innocent dance party to an all out war in Cabrini Green. Butch had the feds roll in with tanks and SWAT."

"Right and they still haven't recovered from all of that. The place got worse because of the mess he made over there. That sumbitch is psycho-loco once he gets spun up."

"Understand. But he has access to all the resources needed especially when it comes to Mob activity."

"Oh well. There goes the neighborhood."

"Just go see Darnell and help him feel better. The road to perdition is paved with blood now."

"Screw you and all your poetic babble blab bro. After this, I'm going to Belize where there ain't no Mob, racists, dope, gangs and SWAT. Just golden beaches, brain coral, and mermaids."

"Ha! You do that little brother. I'll be right behind you. Dad would be proud of us."

"For what?"

"For caring about others enough to get involved and trying to make a difference. Like he did. Jim and Cora Pope were the greatest."

"Fosho bro. Fosho. They were one of a kind, unique. I'll let you know what I find."

"Thanks lil'bro. I'll be waiting for your call. The team will be on the ground soon."

CLICK

CHAPTER 2

GANG OF 8

South of town, down where the Salt Creek and Deer Creeks intersect, three-hundred acres are home to seven recreational lakes. The water fun home for Lincolnites is where sandy beaches bleed into cool clear summer waters or frozen black ice in the winter.

Major League Baseball infields, PGA Golf course sand traps, concrete companies, interstate highways, playgrounds, lakefront resort beaches, and even flamingo zoo habitats, are filled with the sand and gravel quarried from these once productive gravel pits of the Lincoln Sand and Gravel Company.

Discovered by engineer Wyndham C. Jones in 1905 underneath the surface of the Decatur, Springfield, Pekin, Peoria, Bloomington-Normal and the Champaign-Urbana regions of Central Illinois, the massive pits have produced more than 25-million tons of sand and gravel.

After closure of the operation, the seven large deep quarries were filled with water. The 300-acres are now known as the Lincoln Lakes Recreational Area and Sub-Division Community. Ski boats turn up wakes with frolicking summer vacationers from around the Central Illinois region. Lincoln locals rely on the lakes for an anytime get-a-way to the water, a day cook-out or weekend camping and fishing excursions.

Swimmers can dive from an anchored platform 50-yards off shore of one of the lakes. A twenty-foot water slide and dive platform where swimmers perform insane jumps, flips and mega-splashes, is centered at the middle of the lake. Water skiers turn and burn in another lake while anglers cast lures into the heavily stocked fishing lakes. In cold winters, frozen black ice provides a wonderland of speed-skating, twilling and twirling, and creating lasting memories.

Two days after the shootings, a Schafer 510 Sport Pininifarina 50-foot ultra-modern pleasure boat dropped to idle speed. It slowly approached a 100-foot long dock behind a lakeside mansion owned by Barron "Barnie" Barnstone, the richest man in Logan County.

Coming alongside the dock to tie down, Barnie saw a bevy of men waiting for him.

"Well ain't this a lovely view. So you can assemble when called," Barnie scowled as he bounded off of his luxury lake boat before it was secured to the dock. Barnie lead the group of eight through his manicured back yard and patio bar area.

"Somebody tell me what in the name of hells fuck is going on right now! This was not the plan. ANYBODY?! Who shot them? We know it wasn't him." Barnie stomped his way through the group directly to the outdoor bar.

"It better not be one of those greasy mob fucks." LaDarius Knauri pounded his cane on the ground.

"Sheriff? Anything?" Barney looked to Tucker for something to add.

"Hell, I don't know. He was in shock when I picked him up in the street holding the gun. Like he was in a daze but looking for someone, probably the shooter."

"This shit ain't good!" Barnie paced in a panic like a hungry jaguar.

"Keep your toupee on Barnie. This can be a good thing for us." McDougle removed his black skinny brim hat with a sinister scowl.

"The hell you talkin about Red?" Mayor Bartmiester pushed Tucker to the side.

"Think about it. Now we don't have to wait on him to get the will transferred to him before he gets off'ed much later by the Outfit. Hell, we can even get these dirty fuckers out of the deal since someone else has done the work for them." McDougle looked at each man for awareness.

"That won't set well with them." Barnie paced with anger. He grabbed a bottle from the bar.

"The hell with them! They come down there with their mess. Demanding shit. Girls, coke, shine. I'm sick of cow-towing to them greasy dumb Italian fucks." LaDarius stared down the group with a hard gaze pounding his cane on the ground.

"Hey, they're not our problem. They can fuck off. For all we know, they're probably behind all this other shit going on around here anyway." Jeff Ladder removed his jacket as the heat began to rise, even though its the middle of winter.

"Well I wouldn't go that far, not yet anyways. After all, they are in on most of the land deals coming once this thing kicks off. Why would they jeopardize all of this for some petty get back? Jezus man! I had to go through them on most of the union contracts we worked on to secure their construction companies, cement, gasoline, carpenters, a bunch of shit, when all the development begins," McDougle paced the patio, his wild red hair and face glowed with fire.

"So then how do we get rid of them?" Barnie asked.

"I have so much dirt on'em, I can work'em out of the deal." McDougle tried to ensure the group.

"Dream on Red. You flirting with suicide or what?" the tall lanky eldery LaDarius pointed his shakey cane at McDougle.

"I will need to get a murder conviction on the coon. But I will ensure them that it's no problem and that the money will still be good with Darnell out of the way earlier than planned because I will now be the legal executor of the will. I will get one of their prosecutors on the case. He can go for the death penalty on two pre-med murder-one charges. I'm sure the little murderer shows his black ass enough around here to get that to stick."

"The hell you saying Red? You know he didn't shoot'em." Barnie poured a full glass of Old Grand Dad 100 with an unsure hand.

"Yea Red. You talking about railroading the kid?" Bartmeister stepped forward.

"Look. This is our chance to get the entire kit and kaboo-tle. We don't need the Outfit to move on these contracts for development. We can get our own. I know the perfect prosecutor for this. This thing just dropped in our laps. We get the conviction and the death penalty, the kid is gone. Poof!" McDougle snapped is fingers.

"What about appeal?" Barnie said over a swig.

"He certainly cannot afford an attorney. I know all these state defense attorneys around here. I can get them to turn no problem. No one knows about the will except us now. I can ensure a great payoff for anyone of them will be life changing. This my boys is, how the niggers say, is a slam dunk," a red McDougle grinned like Satan.

"The press will be brutal. Frying a kid?" Sheriff Tucker removed his cowboy hat and wiped his brow with a nervous backhand.

"What kid? He'll be 18 on January first. That means an adult conviction. I'll put him in solitary as a suicide risk. That'll break him after a year or two. The press will be gone by then. You know they just move on with these things. Especially with them shines. Hell, they're so many of them inside the fed pens by to do the work, it's no longer a concern. White folks don't care. Blacks have no power to litigate release. So we just keep packing the prisons. We'll have so many of them in the

Illinois peniel system to use as free labor for the projects when they start rolling in. Don't need the Outfit controlling all that labor. Even have the coon-kid working on the projects while he awaits the gas chamber in 10-years. Win-win! We just have to be on the same page when they come-a-knocking. Can you all handle a year, 18-months tops of being in the spotlight?" McDougle paced the group, pushing for buy-in.

They looked at each other with questionable concern. Eyes searched each others for affirmation or disapproval.

"C'mon! This is our chance to launch this state into the economic stratosphere, now! And all of you, my fine fellas, of the right, you'll be lords of your own monopolies. I'm talkin generational wealth for us all!" McDougle going for the knockout.

"But he's just a kid Red! You want to put him through all of that?" Jeff Ladder threw his hands up.

"Trust me, ultimately this world won't give two shits a fuck about another dead nigger. Especially after we shred him in court and demonstrate his angry South Side violent nature. After all, one monkey don't stop no show." McDougle poured his glass of the OG100, neat.

"But he's not like that Red." LaDarius pushed.

"Well GOT DAMNIT this is what you all are here to do! Make this little black angel into a black demon! And figure it out like your lives depend on it!

You all control these friggin rednecks down here, right!? Well then make your people believe the lie. Hell, y'all say it often enough, they'll start to believe it. If all of you run around talkin it up at every farm, bar, barber shop, restaurant, VFW hall, wherever…they *will* buy in. The media will eat that shit up and all that goody-two-shoes shit will be gone. POOF! Our jury will be set. But this needs to happen yesterday." McDougle glared at each one of them as he uttered each word for affect.

The gang of eight started to nod in agreement. Thinking of when, where, and how to spread the Big Lie.

"So you in or you out? I ain't got all night. The fuck you all say? Determine your own future? Or let them greasy ginny wop bastards and a niggers own your pink pimply asses? I thought you were civic leaders? I put all my shit out there for you dickheads for five plus years. Now it's time for you all to get your asses to work and get what is rightfully yours, and get it now! Don't wait for a gift from Mr. Darnell Whitaker, the richest boot in the state, to give you a hand out! You were born and bread here. Pure as the white Jesus-driven snow. Don't stand there and tell me you won't do whatever it takes to defend your families. Next thing you know, them coons will be running Lincoln and enslaving your children and grandchildren. They just waiting for the right moment to take over. Payback for slavery and shit. All that revolutionary talk they do. If you are true Patriots of the Mid-West then you ride or die in the Mid-West defending your families to the seat! It's us or them now! And there's more of us. So let's get what we deserve! What God Almighty intended for us in the beginning." McDougle's high volume energized his right fist to pump at them.

"Fuck yea!" Tucker shouted thrusting his glass of OG in the air.

"Cheehooo!" LaDarius followed.

"Fuckit! I'm not going down like that!" Ladder joined.

The men nodded and agreed with each other. Pounding shoulders in affirmation. Setting the pact, circling, snorting like bulls. Scratching and stomping the ground in their ostrich skin boots.

The eight Lincoln leaders transformed into one colluding spin machine with their eyes firmly set on the +1,000,000 acre prize in what usually is a quiet Central Illinois community.

No silence on the Lincoln Lakes today.

Lincoln Lakes

https://www.adi.org/ourtimes/1999/Summer1999Lakes.pdf

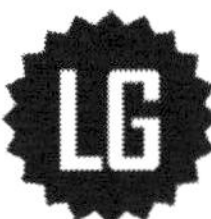

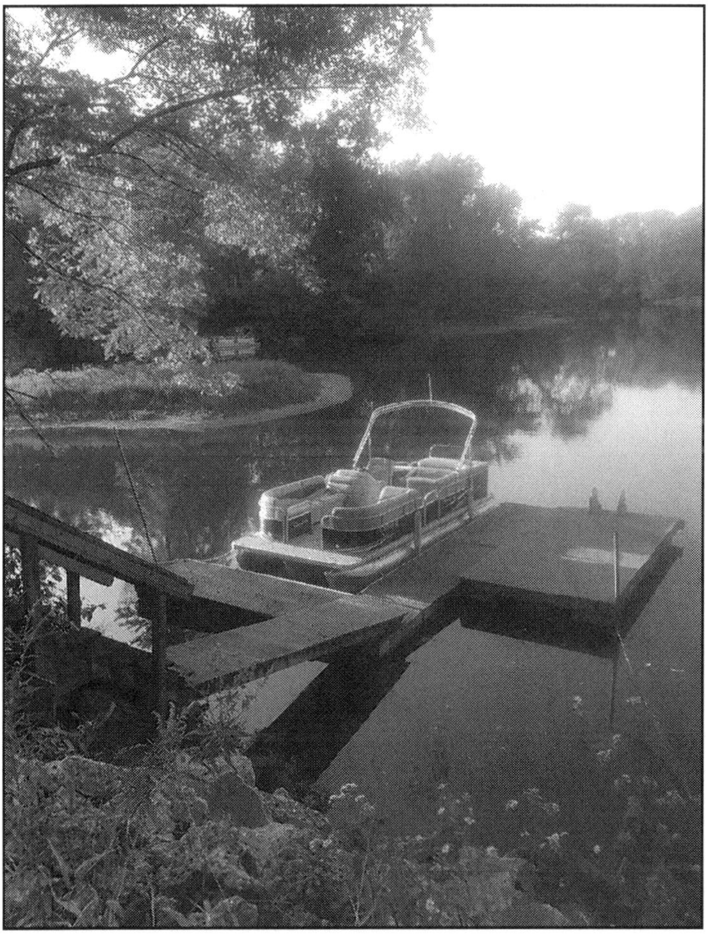

CHAPTER 3

FUNERAL

Old Union Cemetery
December 6th, a mild winter

About three miles south of town on Old Rt. 66, the Old Union Cemetery is the first cemetery in Lincoln and home to resting places of many locals dating back to the 1830s. Lincoln's most notables lay to rest there including; Robert Latham, town founder and friend of Old Abe; Aaron Dyer, escaped slave and Springfield conductor of the Illinois Underground Railroad; his son William Dyer, one of the nation's first African-American physicians and first African-American drafted in WWI; along with many Civil War veterans. The notorious figure of the Prohibition era, John Schwenoha or Coonhound Johnny, the bootlegger, coonhound breeder and cohort to Al Capone. (Historical facts)

The silent home of thousands of ancient oak and ash trees wrapped their muscular low hanging limbs down and around the ancients of Logan County. The powerful guardians towered over the sleeping ancients, shading their eternal homes. In the dappled shade, a rumble of more than 100 cars and trucks awoke the dead. Entering through the flaking rusted iron gates, the long procession filtered its way into the deepest most sacred areas of the resting spirits. Deeper in, daylight was swallowed by the dark matter of the forest guardians. The line of parked cars released the foot procession of mourners who assembled a march behind two black hearses. Like monks to temple, they slowly and deliberately filed down the long shaded path. Deeper in still, the crunching sound of feet and tires on the leafy gravel path was swallowed into the belly of the dark solemn tunnel. Terminating at a sun-bathed circular clearing, the procession entered the resting place of the Abe Lincoln ancients. Now the new home for Chuck and Elizabeth Wagner.

Gravestones formed a concentric pattern that circled the sun-drenched clearing. A ring of headstones were perfectly arranged in twelve inner circles, that created rows directed to the middle, like spokes of a wheel; a very precise Stonehenge-like design. At the center of the circular pattern, a grand shiny black granite stone disk, twenty-feet wide in circumfrence, stood four feet above the gravestones, drawing in the dead from all spokes of the wheel.

Engravings of the names of Abe Lincoln's descendants were carved into the face of the twenty-foot wide circular stone base. The newly chiseled names of the Wagners popped out like white chalk on a blackboard. The various shades of black, gray, blue, green and red specs in the granite, twinkled in the sunlight. A 20-foot tall inverted cone of smooth gleaming black obsidian volcanic stone set atop the circular granite base. The pointed tip of the glimmering black cone was capped with three feet of solid gold. The golden tip sparkled a refracting golden aura from all sides, moving with the sun. The mirror-like black volcanic glass stone absorbed and reflected the suns gleaming heat around the circle of ancients, watching, covering, and warming their souls.

The glimmering black obsidian cone channeled light energy up into the gold point, conducting the sun's beams into a golden heavenly laser. The particle beam created an Inter-

Heaven Highway for the ancient spirits to come and go. Like a sun dial, now pointing a shadow over the Wagner's plots.

The mourners created a thick circle around the perimeter of the site in seance. The entire town seemed to be there: Barbara Sizemore, Howard McDougle and Robert Todd Lincoln Beckwith, the only remaining descendants of Honest Abe. Jayne Gorham, Chuck's sister, clutched bunches of brilliant white lilies against her body. Dressed in all black, the four stood over the twin golden caskets of Chuck and Liz Wagner.

The circular sea of black-hatted Lincolnites from all walks was a Lincon who's who including: Professor Paul Beaver, Historian Paul Gleason, U.S. Congressman Edward Madigan, Governor James Thompson, Civic Leader LaDaris Knauri, land baron Bernardo "Barnie" Barons, Lincoln Courier Managing Editor William Martinie, Banker Raymond Keys, Postmaster Floyd Durst, Tourism Director Jeoffrey Laddish, Mayor Marvin Bartmiester, land baron Joe Funk, Reverend Arthur Neitzell, Fire Chief Jim Habovic and his many firefighters. Sheriff Gabe Tucker, Restaurateur Ernie Edwards and Fay and Tom from the Deep Roots Café, Basketball Coach Edwin McGhee, School Superintendent Dr. Robert Jones, Lincoln High Principle Michael Durso, and Science Professor Dr. Dennis Campbell.

The black mass nestled in harmony around the ancient's spirits and under the giant oak guardians. A teary Maria began linking the circular mass arm-in-arm, including their black fiends; Pit Master Von Brown, Pastor Stan Greenwood and his twin sons Stanley and Stephen, Deputy Mayor Desmond Pope, Norm Cook and his son Brian, along with the entire high school basketball team. Cora Silver, Carolyn Bankhead, Wayne Johnson, Officer Bruce Butler, Ric Miles, Mark and Eddie Brooks, Wyndell Williamson, Bill Malone, and radio DJ John Ellison, who came down from Chicago's station WVON.

Lincoln College professors; Music Professor Robby Cruz, Pre-Med Professor Doctor Mikela Ianthomas, Law Professor Dr. Vera Abbott, Journalism Professor Lorraine Mayo, and Art Director Dr. Addonis Parker. Even Kelvin Reese was there representing the African Israelites. All linked arm in arm.

After Reverend Arthur Neitzell gave the eulogy, Barbara, Jayne, McDougle and Robert Todd Beckwith, laid the lilies atop the twin gold caskets. The funeral director signaled the lowering of the caskets. The black mass circle began to hum and move counter clockwise around the site. As they all moved around the site, grave attendants lowered the two caskets down into the earthen openings. After three rotations, the lead in the rotating circle guided the snaking line inside of the headstone matrix, towards the twin graves. As each person arrived at the fresh open graves, they scooped two fists full of rich Lincoln DNA soil from the fresh dirt pile next to the 6x6x6 grave opening. They each tossed one fistful of dirt inside each grave on top of the golden caskets. They then rejoined the moving circle-line until the last person tossed dirt and returned to the humming human gear. Three more humming rotations and the circle lead turned toward the dark trail. The mass headed back through the tunnel of the ancient guardians along the crunching path.

After all cars departed the cemetery, the last bird stopped chirping. The breeze slowed. Death's silence crept back in. Clouds split. The gleaming obsidian cone sunbeam laser transport began. The silence of deaths aftermath was disturbed by feet gently crushing dry leaves from within the tree line. The muffled forest echo of trampled cracking twigs and leaves was gingerly absorbed by the stillness of life. Booker, Chick, Jimmy, and Deacon emerged from the shadows of the oaks. Standing over the twin open graves. They reflected, wondered, and planned in silence; respecting the ancients.

- Guardians of the ancestors at Old Union Cemetery

https://destinationlogancountyil.com/
old-union-holy-cross-cemetery

CHAPTER 4

THE LOW

710 5th St.
Lincoln Police Department Lock Up

"Hey everybody won't you lend me your ear
There's something to fear
It's here, and it's clear
Men gettin rich off raping the land
I can't understand
Why we don't take them in hand
Woah, oh lord, I don't want to be their fool no more
I don't want to be their fool no more
Open eyes, but you're sleeping
You best wake up' fore tomorrow comes creeping in
'Fore tomorrow come creeping in"

A staticky AM radio station struggled to push out the Grand Funk Railroad hit single behind officer Bruce Butler's desk. The only black officer in the LPD, Butler kept a loose eye on the open cell door of suspect #1. The only tenant in the lockup.

"Hey kid. You got a visitor."

"Who?"

"Hi Darnell."

"Aunt Barbara!"

"Bruce can I talk alone with Darnell?'

"Of course ma'am. Go right ahead ma'am." Bruce tried to tune the radio and clean up the static.

"Oh sweetie what happened?"

Darnell ran to hug her tightly.

"I don't know. First we were at the movies then this dude tried to rob us and he shot mom and dad."

"Who?"

"I don't know him. Some white dude."

"Ever seen him before?"

"No."

"Ok. Don't say anything to anyone else unless I am with them ok."

"Ok."

"Darnell, listen very carefully. There are forces here that want this to be your fault. They will want to put this on you."

"Me! I didn't do anything!"

"Shhhhhhhhh. Not now. There are people listening. Here is what's going to happen. Tomorrow, someone will come here that's on your side. He is called a defense counsel, ok?"

"Ok."

"I will be with him. You will tell him everything. And just like you helped write the statement for the sheriff the other day…"

"The sheriff is a racist! He said I did it and I will burn for it. He's a liar! He doesn't even know what happened…"

"Shhhhhhhh. He doesn't matter. He's not important. Listen, these walls have ears. I need you to go ghost ok."

"Ghost?"

"Yea. Like a zombie. Don't say anything, to anyone accept me and the counsel, understand?

"Ok?"

"This is very important. Anything you say to anyone will get twisted and used against you. Got it?"

"Yes ma'am."

"How are you?"

"Scared. Hungry. This place stinks like pee."

"What are you afraid of?"

"Huh?"

"What are you scared of?"

"This, all of this. They hate me. And I didn't do anything!"

"Exactly. You didn't do anything so you have nothing, and I mean absolutely nothing to be afraid of. There are many people on your side. Now you must be the strong person I know you are. If anyone can endure something like this, it's you. I believe in you Darnell. I believe you will be freed from this. But in the meantime there's a lot of work that must be done. So you must be like a statue. Ok?"

"I understand. Who's going to help me? Nobody here knows me like that?"

"Not to worry, that's my job. I know you like that. And soon, so will everyone else. Chuck and Liz made the right choice. So don't think any other way. Now is time to honor them with your best. Got it. This is big. Can you handle it?"

"I guess so." Tears began to run down his cheeks.

"Of course you can. Darnell?"

"Yes."

"I love you and I will fight for you no matter the cost. You understand me?"

"Yes."

"There is nothing, and I mean nothing stronger than love. Chuck and Liz loved you so much and so do I and so do others." She started tearing and choking up.

"But the rest hate me."

"Forget them and focus on your team, ok?"

"Team?"

"Yea. Like the Avenge men you talk about."

"The Avengers?"

"Right. Them. I'll get you food. You get rest the best you can. What would T'Challa do?"

"He would fight."

"Then we fight. I am the Dora women." She smiled at him sweetly.

"Dora Milage?"

"Yea, them chicks you told me about. Bad asses right?"

"This is a serious struggle Aunt Barbara."

"If there's no struggle there's no progress."

Darnell's eyes lit up. Understanding exactly what Barbara was saying. He smirked sitting back in his chair. More comforted now, still full of pain.

"Officer Butler is on your side. He will make sure you are taken care of."

"Ok. I miss mom and dad. That guy is crazy. He shot them for no reason. Why!!"

"Shhhhhhhhh. Bruce? Will you bring Darnell his lunch now please.? The Texas Chili, Funyuns and pineapple soda, just like we discussed."

"Yes ma'am, on it."

"See you soon Darnell. Remember what we talked about. We fight. And when we fight, we win, ok."

They hugged tightly, reassuring each other. Darnell quietly reflected on all of this.

CHAPTER 5

LINCOLN SHAKE DOWN

Top floor of Jacob's Clothier on Broadway St.

An illegal off-track betting parlor above Jacob's store is suspending operations for an emergency meeting with twenty-five or so locals who play the books at Jacob's; including some of Lincoln's more colorful characters. Fat Freddy, Albert 'Putz" Jones, Harry Dial, and Pops Gillets.

Barney Barnstone called the meeting to speed up the lie about Darnell's guilt. Barney has this group in his pocket as many of them owe him money for gambling loan debts, shine credit, and other dealings.

"Listen up. You all know this kid, the Wagner's so-called experimental kid, right? And you know he killed Chuck and Liz in cold blood, right?. So I need you all to understand this cold blooded killer is a threat to our community, our way of life. We cannot allow him to just cruise on back to his slum life in Chicago with Chuck and Liz's blood on his hands," Barney opened the meeting pacing the room.

"So you think he actually killed them?" Pops Gillets stood.

"Absolutely and Sheriff Tucker told me he practically confessed. But I know there are some people around here who think this kid's shit don't stank. He running around here like he some kind of angelic superstar. Well, we all know these ghetto babies are all flawed. His little act didn't fool me one bit. I was waiting for something to happen and now this horrible thing. I feel so responsible for all of it. Agreeing to have him here. It's my fault." He tried to choke himself up while holding his head down for effect. "We must ensure that the people of this community understand his little ghetto game is over!"

"Barney, I've been around Darnell many times and he never showed any bad signs. He's the sweetest and smartest kid I know around here," Cozy Mae Wells sat up in her chair."

"Now Cozy, I'm no sucker. And the sheriff ensured me that he has all the evidence he needs to convict him of murder-one, twice. I know he's been in and out many ya'lls houses and what not. But I been hearing rumbles that he was threatening blow up the town and calling out people as racists and what not. Maybe in a crowd he shines, you know how greasy they are. In closed quarters it's been said that he's sinister. Has some kind of silver bullets. I think they missed the sociopathic part when they was evaluating him. He very city-slick. Taking advantage of our, farm-life goodness."

"Yea. Craig Gilbeaux was mopping the floors at the sandwich shop when he heard him threatening folks. He said he overheard him talking about shooting people in the head. Liz and Chuck were trying to calm him down," Putz Jones looked around the room for support.

"Ya see folks. Spread the word around your dinner table, in your barns, at the barber shops, in your church. Let your God fearin people know that Lincoln needs to cleanse itself of this cancer. He spread his disease into all of us with his goody two-shoes act. He was concocting his master plan all along. He thought there were no witnesses. All the tragedy that has happed lately, WAS HIM I TELL YA! You remember when he came here. Didn't want to be here. Some say he was hiding his hate for Chuk and Liz. They say he was acting and had a secret plan. This is unprecedented in our community. These people are a poisoning our blood. He lured Chuck and Liz in that alley cuz he knew there would be no witnesses back there. You know that alley is sealed off from you being able to see all the way in there. Just like he burned down Jays house and the daycare. He a smart little bastard ya no. You seen how cunning he is. He probably hid the gun in there then he struck like a viper. Cold, heartless. I mean, he had the gun in his hand when Gabe arrested him, right!" Barney walked amongst his congregation of debtors, now converted into doubters.

The room went silent. They looked at each other partly conflicted, partly convinced. Barney set the hook.

"Well he did show his true colors at the college one day when Old Abe's great great grand son was speaking. Blatant disrespect I tell ya. I was there. He was so disrespectful to Judge McDougle. Especially after what Red has done for that kid, basically saving his life," Fat Freddy added.

"Thats right. I was there for that ugly display too. Think of the tourists who will not come here knowing that we, the fine people of Lincoln, allowed a killer to run loose in our community. People will be afraid to come here. No hotel rents. Restaurants go down. Think of the revenue we'll loose. Remember, we gotta prove to the state that we are a good and pure community if we are going to get gambling legalized here again like back in the day."

"Yea! Make Lincoln great again!" Shouted Harry Dial.

"We can't afford to have another Illinois shake down here in Lincoln again like back when. We haven't come this far to make sure the little guys don't lose. If we want to take our town back to the glory days, where slots were king, then we must protect our image." Putz Jones chimed in.

"Yea!" Belted out from several others.

"Harry. You were there back in 1950 when they raided Swiggles Tavern and Moose Lady."

"Yea and they hit Eagles, the Elks Lodge, and the VFW. They even took down the American Legion! Ripped out all of Coon Hound's Indian slots!" Harry Dial huffed shaking his finger at the group.

"They made us pay taxes on the slot machines that they said are illegal! How you suppose to pay taxes on something that's illegal?" Fat Freddy fueled the crowd more.

"So listen up folks. You see where we're headed if we get this black mark on us. Our future is at stake. We have the right to our happiness. Are you happy here playing the books? Of course you are. No hassles right? We all know the big picture. I'm doing my damnedest to get this gambling thing overturned and back in play again. You all know this! I'm for all of you! I want what you want. We clean this mess up, we on easy street with the state gambling commission. So you all do your part and I will do my part. Ok? Matter of fact, if all of you here do your part and we get this kid outta here, then all ya'llz debts with me will be reduced or even erased. You have my word on that. That's how committed I am to you, my people. This kid ain't turning Lincoln into his Ghetto!" Barney amped up the group higher.

Operation Big Lie underway.

- Taking their town back to the good ole days

Part 2

GATHERINGS

CHAPTER 6

CONFESSION

The jingle of keys and clanking cell door startled Darnell. Officer Butler Butler poured a cup of coffee for him.

"Hey kid. You awake? Howd you sleep?"

"Eh."

"You drink coffee?"

"No."

"That's all I have now, sorry. I can put lots of milk and sugar in it."

"Sure."

"I'll get your breakfast a little later. How you holding up?"

"This sucks."

"Understand. I'm really sorry about all this kid. Between me and you, I know you didn't do this. But you got great people helping you."

"Then why am I here?"

"Just the process. But don't worry. Anything you need, I gotchoo. Cool?"

"Thanks. Man your boss is out of control. I thought police are suppose to be the good guys, at least down here. I don't expect anything good from them up in Chicago. But here? Man, dang."

"Yea. I came down here from the Evanston PD to get away from all that bullshit. But this place is mostly cool, especially the people. Regular folks. There's always a few bad apples. And the politics and good ole boy system is well in play. I'll do my best to keep the vultures away from you. You have my word."

"Cool. Thanks officer Butler."

"Call me Bruce. By the way, you have a visitor. Come on down to the holding room."

Darnell came to the interview table where someone was waiting.

"Hey kiddo. How are you?" Dez Pope greeted him.

"Hey Dez. Not so good. Need Luke Cage bout now. Bust through these walls."

"Yea. Dr. Strange could change this whole reality. I'm so sorry my man. I brought you these classics though, Luke, Falcon, Green Lantern, Surfer…"

"I don't get it Dez."

"What?"

"Why? Why this guy shoots mom and dad. What did they ever do but all the right things?"

"Who was it?"

"I don't know. Some stupid kid, drunk. He was trying to rob us. I think He…I'm not spose to say anything. Aunt Barbara told me not to say anything to anyone."

"I understand. I'm as upset as you are. This is not the kind of place where this happens. I just need to know you're ok. Officer Bruce only let me in here cuz I'm the deputy mayor, his boss. Your aunt Barbara is so upset. She's calling in the friggin National Guard on this."

"Huh?"

"Well not the actual National Guard but she's been on the phone yelling at everyone to get on this and find out the truth. Man, she knows everybody. Don't worry, you gonna have the best team representing you. The friggin Avengers be coming to town once she gets done with it."

"That's good."

"Hey, keep your chin up. The normal people know you didn't do this."

"Yea well I now see there are more abnormal people in town than I thought."

"Look, you just told me it was some punk kid. When the Wayne parents were gunned down in the alley, which by the way was next to a theater playhouse, wow, crazy coincidence… that punk kid thought he would get away with it too."

"Yea but little Bruce Wayne was not tagged for the murder."

"True. But you know as much or little about this jerk as Bruce did. And he was able to avenge their deaths. Look what happened to him."

"Yea. I spose."

"So what else can you tell me about this dude?"

"That's enough sir!" A voice came from behind him.

"Who are you?"

A high power looking tight suit wearing black woman came in the room quickly shutting down the conversation.

"I'm his counsel. Darnell don't say another word to this man."

"I'm the Deputy Mayor ma'am. And who are you exactly?"

"I'm JC Monroe. From Mathew, James and Desmond, attorneys at law, Chicago.

"Oh, cool name, Desmond. Well me and Darnell go way back and I was just…."

"You were just leaving sir! Thank you. We will take it from here."

"UNCLE CHICK, UNCLE JIMMY! What are you doing here!?"

Darnell hugged the two uncles as Dez quietly left the room scowling at officer Butler on his way out.

"We here for you D. We on the team to get you outta here and back home." Jimmy came to him with a hug.

Darnell's hug gripped both men with the strength of Luke Cage and the affection of Mamma G.

"Darnell I'm here on behalf of your lead defense counselor to gather as much information as we can to build your case. So I think we should get started.

Have a seat, ok?" JC pulled out his chair.

"You said on behalf of? On behalf of who?"

JC looked at Chick and Jimmy then to Darnell.

"Um your lead counselor is one million percent behind you. He is one of Chicago's top defense attorneys."

"Why is he behind me? How does he know me? Doesn't this cost money? I don't have any money."

"You don't need money." JC stared at him deeply. Hoping he would not ask more about the mysterious attorney.

"OK. But how do you know Uncle Chick and Jimmy? How did you all know about this? So fast?"

"Um. Well…"

"Yo D. No bullshit. Your father is your lawyer. He knows everything."

"What!!"

"Jimmy!!" JC hollered at him.

"Hell wit all dat. We here now! Percy is in this 100%." Jimmy stepped to Darnell.

"Yea Darnell. Your father is a brilliant bad ass mo-frikkin Chicago lawyer. He's angry as fuck and laser-focused on this, on you. He'll get you outta here." Chick stepped closer to him.

"I don't need his help! I don't want it! Get somebody else! What about Aunt Barbara?"

"Um, she's not a lawyer Darnell." JC tried to say with concern.

"Look here D. Straight up ok? Percy has known about all of this since day one." Jimmy pulled up a chair but did not sit.

"Uh Jimmy you shouldn't say any…"

"Naw, fuck that! This shit real now. We done with all this hocus-pocus shit!

Look here D, your father is the baddest sum bitchin lawyer on the South Side.

White boys scerd of 'hm. He got plenty brothers off from bogus charges like-a-mug for years now. He knows errything about you, all this. He put your mother in the best medical re-hab facility in the state. He's still hurtin over all of that. He been paying your bills since the day he left."

"Well he should! He shouldn't have left!"

JC comforted him, touched his arm gently. "Ever since that night of the fight, he went straight to work getting you everything you need to succeed. He even got you into Mamma Gs. That's why you stayed there so long. Then when this adoption thing came up, he and I worked diligently on delaying the law for interracial adoption until you were 18, so you wouldn't get selected. But some underhanded legislators passed the law in the middle of the night and they rushed to get you adopted by the Wagner's."

"But why?" Darnell searched all of their eyes.

"That is the question many many many people have been working on ever since you were moved. And I do mean many people Darnell. All of it lead by your father. He truly is dedicated to you Darnell, in ways you don't know but you will."

"Why didn't he say anything to me?"

"He knows how you feel about him. It tears at his soul. He didn't want to fight you. He only wants to facilitate the best opportunities for your future. That is what motivates him. He's dedicated his life to getting you put in the best situations while he established himself as a lawyer, even when he wanted to quit law school after the fight. He even went to jail for a time trying to pay for your needs. He was incredibly depressed. But you motivated him to stay in the fight more than anyone else. You Darnell, you are his fire and everyone knows it back home and they are supporting him and you."

Darnell stared down at his Chuck Taylors, contemplating it all.

"And D. Me and Jimmy have had a team here in Lincoln since you got here. We been on your tail since jump street. We been on the low low." Chick moved in even closer to him.

"Huh?"

"Yea, almost since day one we been here. Ain't missed a lick on black stick. The fair, basketball practices, water skiing, the jazz jams, the pig farm, the hay rides, corn shucking, rodeo, cuddling with those alpacas, axe throwing, cookouts at the house, chili cook off, movies with the girl…damn boy she fine too bruh…all of it, ya'no? We been on you like white on rice. I was even in the toilet stall next to you when you threw up all that fried food at the fair." Chick smiled.

"And we were there when the shots were fired in the alley. But when we got to Liz and Chuck and that cook from the bar, you had gone. When I ran through the alley after you, the cop put you in the car." Jimmy moved in closer to him.

Darnell's eyes widened with surprise.

"Yep. But we stayed on the serious low-low everyday. We didn't want to blow our cover or get you hemmed up." Chick put his hand on Darnell's shoulder.

The three closed in to his personal space. JC looked at Darnell sweetly, searched for his reaction. Darnell looked up with a hard scowl seemingly about to explode. He saw six loving eyes looking down at him. He studied them intently. Shifted from one set of eyes to the next. Their sweet yet serious expressions of love and concern gazed through him. He opened his mouth but nothing came out. A tear slid down his cheek. JC teared up, sniffled, crossed her arms and rubbed her goosebumps hoping for his acceptance. Inching in ever closer to him, Darnell stood, paused, then lunged into her with a great and wanting hug. All four group-hugged in a silent embrace.

"This is only part of your team." JC announced.

"Part?"

"There are many more here and at home. There is one more person who will act as your counsel with me and your father. He will be providing us with critical legal assistance needed to get you outta here."

"Who is he? Where is he?"

"He'll be here. Shall we begin?"

"Not without me!"

Barbara Sizemore entered the room.

"That's my sister that son of a bitch just killed. His ass is mine."

CHAPTER 9

LEGAL BRIEF

Logan County Court House

"Now where I come from we don't give a damn
We do whatever we please
It ain't about no downtown, nowhere bound
narrow mind drag
It's all about being free
Everybody's going uptown
It's where I want to be
Uptown
You can set your mind free
Uptown
Keep your body hot
Get down
I don't want stop"

Sir, your four o'clock, Mr. Frongello is here."

"Thank you Carolyn. Send him in. Be sure to put Mr. A's call through as soon as he calls. Don't let him wait. I need to speak with him ASAP. And turn down that radio." McDougle forcefully punched the intercom button with edgy irritation.

Paralegal Carolyn Bankhead rolled her eyes and did not respond. She turned up the Prince jam a tiny bit more on her radio. McDougle's treatment of her was coarse on a daily basis. She just dealt with his ways.

The only black professional legal aid in the courthouse, she has been tolerating McDougle for seven years. Including through her legal studies at Lincoln College night school, and now this job. She maintains her calm demeanor with him, never giving too much. Never overreacting to his insufferable rants and sexist comments.

"Bob. Come in. How was the train ride?" McDougle stood to greet the Mob prosecutor for the Whitaker case.

"Fantastic Red. Never gets old. The smell of pig shit through the cornfields for three hours from the city. Who could tire of that?" He forced a chuckle.

"Don't get snippy with me Bubbles. This is the big one. Just be glad the Don called you and not that worm Chertofs. He burned his bridges."

"I think ole Skelator is not doing well."

"Doing what well? Asshole couldn't win a case if it was handed to him. Speaking of a hand job, you have all the discovery I sent you, right?"

"Yes judge. Thank you. I certainly hope so. We should be able to open and shut this mooley in two days."

"My my, aren't you feeling your meatballs." McDougle poured two glasses of Beefeaters and tonic.

"No witnesses of the act. The weapon in hand. Plenty of eye-witnesses to prove motive and intent. Haven't had a murder-one in years. This'll be like ole times back in the Bobby Seale Black Panther days. Hope we get to gag this kid like we did Seale. That was epic. The crap you pulled back then Red, just epic. We were one helluva team." Frongello sipped from his glass.

"Yea, that seems like eons ago Bubbles. When I say we have a slam dunk here, I mean a SLAM DUNK. Like Big Wilt. So listen, Don Niccolo Anaganino is really getting heat from the Vatican. But this gift we have been handed puts us in the home stretch. We get this right, and we will, we are home free. Contracts in place. Legislators on board. This is basically handed to us on a golden platter."

"Yea, never liked the taste of silver spoons. I can see my early retirement seven figures. And money too. Ha ha! The seven virgin figures will be my reward!" Frongello sucked down his gin and tonic with joy.

"You one crazy bastard Bobby. So let's get down to business."

"Red you know who is on the team from Mathew, James and Desmond, right?"

"Yes."

"You know who's their top attorney right?"

"Yea, Whitaker."

"Red. He's the kids father."

"Yes! This will be epic Frong!"

"How so?"

"This will go down in history as our finest hour Frong. We get the kid. The father will be humiliated. He breaks down and eases off you guys in the city. You have leverage. Love it." McDougle sips the Beef.

"He's been making noise in Chicago Red. You been tied up down here and in Springfield too long. He's been needling away at the Outfit. He and his Nigger Jew Spick team have their noses in our shit at every turn. But we turn them back. But they have laid out so much on us already. I don't like where it's headed. They are playing the long game on us. Smacks of New York and Gotti."

"No problem. I remember that gorilla mother fuckin smart mouth at Law School. Who does he think he is? Billy D. Williams? I fianlly have him now?"

"What do you mean Red?"

"Been after this ass-hole ever since Northwestern. Now I can really drive a stake in his black ass. I've been wanting him out of my life since he first walked into my classroom. Uppity-ass nigger. Thinks he can do the law from the ghetto.

Now I can finally destroy him. I thought ripping his kid away was the stake to drive in his heat but this is so much better. Perfect." Red downs his gin and tonic. Eats the entire lime wedge. Peel and all.

"Ok Red, whatever you say. Shall we begin?"

McDougle and the Mob prosecutor go over their alternate facts of the case they will ram through the court with McDougle's plunger. He gave Frongello detail after detail as to how they will get the murder-one charge to stick as they devise a coordinated plan to cover their bases of burden of proof against Darnell.

Red assisted Frongello in drafting his opening statement so it aligns with his opinion to come. Making an open and shut case all the more likely. McDougle's local cohorts are lining up witnesses and their stories. Forensic experts from Springfield have the gun, pulling Darnell's finger prints, smudging Russell's. His tentacles reaching deep into the Illinois State and Logan County justice systems to ensure all roads lead to a swift guilty verdict.

"Excuse me sir, the WGN reporter is on line three again. You want to take it this time?" Carolyn interrupted over intercom.

"Damnit. That bitch is still snooping around?"

"Does she know anything?" Frongello asked.

"Hell no."

"Alright Carolyn."

"I'll talk to you later Red. Thanks again for everything. I'll see my way out."

McDougle waved Frongello off. "Ok. put her through Carolyn…. Mrs. Justone, how are you? What can I do for you?"

"It's Justine and it's more like what I will do for you sir." Her deep peppery lioness voice responded.

"Um, well I guess that depends on what you need Ms. Justine. How can I be of service to your fine organization?"

"Well I'm seeking a statement from you about the Darnell Whitaker case. Do you know what the prosecution is going for? Who is the prosecutor?"

"Well I'm no mind reader so I don't know what is in the head of the prosecutor but on the surface this seems like a tragic and unfortunate event. The young man had everything handed to him and he just destroyed it all. But you know I cannot discuss an on-going investigation or case." McDougle sucked his teeth.

"Of course sir but do you think he committed the murder?"

"Not for me to say. I'm merely presiding over the contest. A glorified basketball referee."

"Oh you are no half court cop sir. You are soooo much more. Surely you have some personal feelings about this case given you helped facilitate the boy's adoption to the Wagner's. Shouldn't you recuse yourself? How can you be impartial?"

"True I did help the family a bit but I'm not perfect. Off the record?"

"Ok sir."

"I obviously made a mistake. The person I thought was an outstanding young man turned out to possibly be a violent killer. Don't know how I missed it. There was always the argument that these kids from these type families are born to lie, cheat and steal. They will say anything to get something for free. I guess he fooled me too. I was merely an administrator, no personal feelings either way. Just doing my job. Ms. Justine, all clients are the same to me. My record proves that."

"So you think he *is* guilty of killing his parents??"

"I didn't say that. But my heart is torn apart as my cousin and her husband have been brutally murdered by a person I helped bring into their lives. I only wanted what they wanted and tried to do my part to help my cousin. I am so torn Mrs. Justine. But I don't know the facts of the case until they are presented in court. I am blind justice. I want justice no matter what it looks like. Umm, can we discuss this later?"

"I understand. It is so sad and must be difficult for you. You sound like you can use a drink. Can I meet you for a non biased off-the-record cool one?

"Well, I hope that would not be an inappropriate liaison."

"Oh no! We can keep it social. You sound so torn. Maybe I can help you feel better? Ya'no, so you can focus on the big picture. We all are under lots of stress now. Lord knows I am feeling the stress of it all from every angle. It makes me so tense and sore."

"Yes, yes. We are. I would love that. Say this evening at 7pm at the Mill? A safe place with good people and cheap drinks."

"Sounds great. I'll get a shower at my room at the Motel Seven and meet you at the Mill."

"Sounds good. Do you have a car? Cabs are not like the city here ya'no. Shall I pick you up?"

"Oh, um…that would be wonderful! I can't imagine a better evening for me than to be picked up by the great Howard McDougle. Secretly you are really large to me. I love to hear you speak. I have followed some of your trials. I'll wear something appropriate to be in your presence."

"Oh no please, you are too kind. Let your hair down. Blue jeans and t-shirt is fine with me. I am surrounded by stuffed shirts all day. I really need to let go tonight."

"Oh thank you. But I have the perfect dress. I call it my purple passion."

"Oh behave."

"Oh Howard."

"Call me Red."

"Mmm. I like that. Red. That's hot. See you at seven. Room 169, Red."

"My favorite number."

"What a coinky-dinky. It's mine too." She giggled.

"See you at seven, Purple Passion."

"I'll be REDeee.'

Click

Desiree hung up the pay phone on the corner of Broadway and S. Mclean St. in front of the Post Office and across the street from the courthouse.

"What he say?" Donovan asked anxiously.

"Seven pm, at the room."

"Perfect. I'll be ready," Donovan rubbed his hands together.

"He's a fuckin greasy lizard. Forked tongue shit. Not even worthy of snake status." Desiree sneered a turned up lip power striding out of the phone booth.

"Girl, you are the best. Got me percolating listening to that sleazy performance." Donovan smiled with the anticipation of a hunter baiting a trap.

"You can't handle this sleaze."

"Can you?"

"Sheeeiiiit. Let's get set up. Frongello will be leaving his office soon. Can't be seen out here on the courtyard grounds."

COURTHOUSE SQUARE
HISTORIC
DISTRICT
700 BROADWAY
100 S. McLEAN

CHAPTER 7

FRONPRICKELLO

O fficer Butler?"

"It's Bruce. C'mon now Darnell. We cool. Sup?"

"Sorry. Do you read comics?"

"Um, not really. Maybe looked at a few Batman and Blade. Gotta get to Dez's place."

"Do you think life is like the comics?"

"What you mean?"

"Ya'no, like super heroes swooping in and saving the day with super powers like no other human?"

"Well, somewhat. Take the police. Most people don't have the skills we do, we train for. So when we show up on a scene, we can do some super things that most people cannot. The power of will."

"Huh?"

"Will power. Will we or won't we? We're trained for the *will we*. Most folks are *won't we*, when it comes to difficult situations. Don't want to get involved or afraid."

"I see. So you think comics are representations of some peoples will to do things others are not capable of."

"Those characters may be super-duper and all, but if *you* saw a kid in a lake struggling to swim out, would you jump in and get the kid?"

"Heck yea!"

"Super duper, ya dig?"

"Hmmm. I see what you mean."

"You thinking you need a super hero now?"

"Well, I know the comics are fiction, dreamed up in a studio somewhere. Maybe I do. But ain't no studio around here to dream up help for me."

"Well you know what happens when the bat signal goes up from commissioner Gordon's roof top?"

"Um, yea."

"Shit happens bro. Big shit. Bad shit. Somebody gets knocked the fuck out and sent to jail shit."

Darnell smiled a bit. Contemplating who his Batman will be.

"Hello? Excuse me officer. I'm looking for Darnell Whitaker?"

"And who are you?"

"I'm Yuri Yendell. I will be on the team representing him."

Officer Butler looked at the somewhat frazzled, underweight, tallish lanky guy in a wrinkled brown herringbone suit sporting black framed glasses and a blue and white yarmulke on his head.

"Um. Ok. He's down here. Come with me this way."

"Yo D. Your super hero just arrived," he whispered as they entered the cell. "Don't judge a book by its cover. Note the Clark Kent's," Butler winked. "This way please gentlemen. Right in here. Just call me when you are done, ok Clarke?" Bruce ushered them into the small meeting room.

"Um, it's Yuri."

"Riiiight," Bruce smiled and walked away.

"Hello Darnell. My name is Yuri, not Clarke. Not sure where he heard that. I distinctly told him my name is Yuri." He tried to smile and comfort Darnell holding out his hand to shake.

Darnell looked him up and down, rolled his eyes then sat behind the table.

"More like the Penguin." Darnell mumbled to himself.

"I'm sorry. I didn't hear you."

"Nothing."

"I am here to represent you as one of your attorneys. I work with attorney JC Monroe and others in our Chicago law firm, and I want to say how honored I am to represent you."

"Where is she? Is she Cat Woman?"

"Um, you mean Ms. Monroe? I…I'm not sure what you mean by cat woman but she is completely involved. She's doing research. Gathering evidence and…ohhhh! Cat Woman. That's right. You're a comic genius, a connoisseur of the craft. I have read so much about your skill-set in the comic arts."

"My what?"

"I understand you are an expert in the universe of comics."

"Oh that. I guess. Not gonna help me now unless you're Dr. Strange."

"No I'm not a Doctor but some say I can be a bit strange."

He fumbled through his big leather brief case. He dropped papers. Struggled to organize his things. Darnell watched his goofy dance, holding his head, more eye rolling.

"Sorry, so much material. Got a little shuffled on the train ride down. Lovely country-side down here. My first time here. Beautiful. And the smells are incredible. The smells of life. The city smells like death."

"You mean that pig pin crappy smell?"

"Ha! Well yes. The smell of sweet success. I guess if we didn't smell that crap then we would be in trouble. No more Sausage McMuffins from Mikey Ds."

Darnell chuckled at that. Remembering his ride from Chicago to Lincoln with Chuck and Liz for the first time. And their stop at Mikey Ds.

"Well time is of the essence so shall we get right to it?"

"To what?"

"Defending you innocence of course."

"Everyone thinks I did it."

"Not on this side of the table. We are convinced you are completely innocent and we intend to prove it."

"Really!" Darnell perked up.

"Yessir. We have people doing plenty of work to find all the evidence leading to your innocence, including the actual killer."

"So you know there is a white dude out there who did this?"

"Oh yes and we intend to find him."

"How?"

"That is the tricky part. But until we do, we are going to make sure your rights are well protected and that these country jurors know you are completely innocent of these charges. As well, we will make sure these police and others know you are innocent. How have the police been treating you?"

"Well other than the sheriff, who is a racist!…

"Um let's not go there right now. We will get to that later."

"Officer Butler is great."

"THAT'S BRUCE!!!!" Butler called out from down the hall.

"Yea, Bruce is great and so is officer Sullivan."

"Good. We are going to take this in steps. So step one. Lets' get to the facts of the case. Me and you build it, load it up then shoot them down."

"Like Silver Surfers's Silver Bullets of Truth?"

"Uhhhh, sure."

Yuri peppered Darnell with questions, getting the minute details. Taking copious notes, asking and re-asking Darnell the same questions. Training him for the trial, ensuring he is consistent with his answers. The discussion goes on for four hours with Bruce bringing them food and drinks from Fay and Tom's Deep Roots Café on the corner of S. Kickapoo and Pulaski St. Darnell got chili with Vidalia onions and ginger beer. Abe, the Reuben sandwich. He insisted they put Swiss cheese on top of the sauerkraut and the Russian dressing before layering the toasted rye on top. He said it reduces spillage, insisting the melted cheese binds the kraut to the fatty edge of the corned beef, sealing in the juices and the sauce. Bruce rolled his eyes at the sandwich science. He agreed to fulfill their requests for pineapple ice cream waffle cones from the Top Hat Creamery on Pulaski St.

They wrapped up the first session around 7pm. Yuri said he will return at 9am to continue. Bruce escorted him out of the jail, he noticed three blobs of Russian dressing and kraut juice stains on his tie. He chuckled. Yuri looked at him wondering.

Leaving the jail, Yuri walked across the street through the courthouse grounds seeing McDougle leaving the building near the corner of Pulaski and Kickapoo Streets.

"Well well. If it isn't Mr. Yendell. What in God's name… err… you do call him God right?…brings you to lil'ole Lincoln? Looking for a job at the kosher deli? Give up on the dream? Chicago too big for you?

"Howard. I see you will be presiding over the Whitaker case. I filed my papers as co-defense counsel with Percy Whitaker and JC Monroe. Shouldn't you recuse yourself, sir?

"And what a team it will be. The three Stooges play Lincoln. Putting the B-team band back together I see. I'm afraid nostalgia is not always the best strategy in law. A little late on filing, Mr. Yendell? Small town's move quickly. Not a large docket here. Had me waiting in chambers for your documents. What, did you walk here from Chicago because of your convictions?"

"Whatever." Yuri scowled at McDougle.

"Don't you worry about recusal. The state legal board and supreme court already approved me to remain. That's how fast it woks down here son. So you and your bush league team, I hope you have employed great paralegals, can rest assured you will receive impartial judicial oversight of this case. This will certainly be an uphill climb for you though. Are you up for the task? A loss doesn't mean you give up the dream. I taught you better than that Mr. Yendell."

"Loss? Sir we haven't even begun the trial and you already have us on the train back to Chicago with our tails between our legs. Sounds like advanced bias to me, sir."

"Oh certainly not! I'm merely stating that loosing is not the end of the world for any attorney. Winning at all cost is what's important for your client. Are you prepared for that?"

"Of course."

"Good. Then I taught you all well. Then I bid you good day sir. I have an engagement to attend. You have a good evening."

"Sir, you realize Percy Whitaker is lead." McDougle froze.

"Ahhh yes. The lazy engine mechanic. Like back in the old days. I am aware counsel. Talk about bias and recusal? Your little hootin-nanny love fest for his little boy won't sway me or the jury. Trust me, I am totally impartial." He beamed laser pupils through Yuri.

"As are we sir."

"Good. I hope your little college prank will not get your client in more trouble. This ain't Northwestern anymore Mr. Yendell. You people are in the big leagues now. No more sleeping in class and taking shabbat on your mommy and daddies dime. I tried to help you student's back then, but I cannot not help you now. I hope you know what you are doing Mr. Yendell. I must go now. Have an engagement."

"Trust me sir, we do. Maybe I will get you some matzah and lox to sooth your inflamed eczema." Mcdougle tightened his lips and turned away. His red ears and forehead began to bloom. They departed in opposite directions making sure they do not look back at each other.

"Dip shit." McDougle murmured.

"Jack-ass." Yuri walked away like McDougle left a fart to linger.

A dark suited attorney-looking figure approached Yuri.

"Excuse me. Are you Yuri Yendell?"

"Yes."

"I'm Robert Frongello, lead prosecutor in the Whitaker trial."

"Oh. Yes I recognize you from TV interviews. Wasn't one-hundred percent sure yet who will prosecute. Glad to know now. How can I help you?"

"Is now a good time to discuss a deal? A plea? You know you don't have a rats chance in hell on this. Your guy is guilty as sin and everyone in this backwater knows it. You'll never get an unbiased jury. I mean, how can your firm afford a lengthy appeal? How long do you want to put this kid through this ringer? How fair is this to him?"

"Are you done?"

"Let's keep this professional shall we? So you're not interested in say, man-two? Two counts, say 30 years? 15 each? Emotional response to his difficult situation? Temporary loss of sanity given the interracial adoption circumstances, yada yada? Come up for parole say, five years? No Super Max. What'dya say?"

"Please counselor. Must we?"

"He's a kid. No need for all this show. Dumb farmer rednecks on the jury. You don't want to upset this tranquil backwater porta-potty down here, do ya? That's not our role. Civil unrest, political fireworks, TV all over the place. Just git'er done and get outta this shit hole and back to the real world. Don't you miss Chicago hot dogs, deep dish pizza, Italian beef, Chicago mix, nice Jewish girls? Get back to the city and get paid for bigger, better, more complex lengthier cases against bigger fish with deep pockets. Bill by the hour. Ya no? What do ya say counselor? I'm sure this is Pro Bono. Or you trying to drain the Wagner's trust fund? Abe Lincoln money in your pockets maybe?"

"Again, are you done? For one, these people are not dumb redneck farmers. They are brilliant life sustainers who you obviously have no respect for. As for your offer, I say no and then hell no! Don't you represent the Outfit anyway? Why do you care about this case? What's in it for them? Thanks for this bit of theater though. I appreciate you opening another door for us. Bring your slime to court with you, please. I will love pointing them out to this lovely backwater community to demonstrate the Outfit's attempt to get a stranglehold on this lovely shit dump, as you call it. Grease them up. Threaten. Extort. Payoffs? You can understand that, right? Why do you care? Ole Donny A-hole getting bored up in the city? Needs to take on meaningless fodder in the boonies? Hmm? Something smells awfully rank around here and it's not the pig shit up the road. I'm sure these lovely little rednecks will love to hear about all that."

"Blow it out your heeb ass Yendell! You fuck with us, you know what happens."

"Hmm, let's see. More extortion cases to try. More Jewish lawyers breathing down your necks opening up more trafficking, tax evasion, bribery, mail fraud, and murder cases against you people. RICO -Land is where you are headed sir. Sure I know exactly what this means. More attention focused on you slimy ass-holes. Perfect. Yea, we'll see you in court, no matter how rigged it will be. We already assume you have your little greasy dicks in this wedding soup. So yea, we will appeal this farce. Then we'll slap you around with our gefilte fish at the state then federal level. Love to see Donny A-Boy in the Illinois Supreme Court. That will be soooo noice! Opening even more slimy doors you people hide behind. Schmucks. Happy now little prick? I'm mean, professional prick. Good day Mr. FronPrickello." Yuri walked away, grinning. "Mazel tov!"

Frongello fumed in silence on the court house grounds.

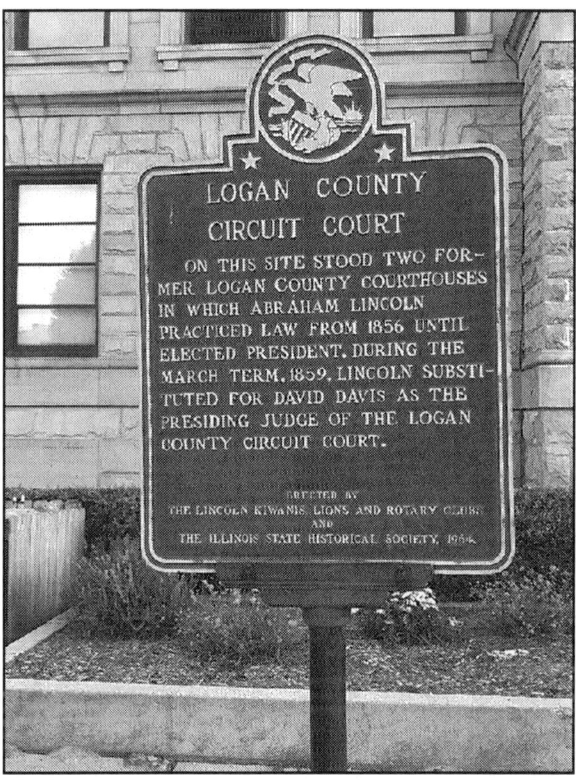

- Courthouse Square, Lincoln Illinois

CHAPTER 8

DREAM TEAM

December 10
Lincoln Train Depot

The screaming Texas Eagle locomotive slowed it's engine to a stop into the Lincoln train station at 4:30 pm. Not many passengers stepped off of the six-car train arriving southbound from Chicago. Most of the passengers arrived on the 8:30 pm stop from the Windy City.

Percy Whitaker strode off of the train with a worried lawyer scowl. Stopping to take in the new air, he looked left, right, then straight as the train pulled away behind him.

"What in the hell is this place? 1950's Mayberry?"

Carrying one bag of luggage and one document-stuffed leather box-case on wheels, he moved with uncertain assuredness down the vacant train platform. The train whistle diminished south and away. The warning bell stopped ringing as the cross bar rose. Cars bounced across the tracks. When the dust settled, he saw the front of the Blue Dog Inn across the street. He made his way to the rendezvous.

"Howdy, I'm Katrina. Welcome to the Blue Dog on Dutch Row. My daddy Rick runs this place now. You came fer deenner?"

"Um, uh sure I'm…"

"Not from here right? Just off the southbound? Must be awful famished. That ride will drain ya sumptin good. You look lak a horseshoe type ta me. Definitely not a Pony. Nope not at'all." She looked him up and down."

"Uh I don't really do horse meat but I'm looking for…"

"Ha! Lord you gotta be from Chicago cuz them St. Louy boys know the deal. Don't choo worry none, we don't eat no Trigger down here baby. Not today anyways! Ha! You married?"

"I'm looking for some colleagues of mine, two men and a woman. Probably look more like me than…"

"Than us local hicks? C'mon. They over'n this-a-way hun. Ask them bout the Pony. They be swearing by it bout now."

"Sure."

Percy shook the cobwebs out of his head wondering which side of Oz he landed in.

"Well, well, well. The gangs' all here. How we looking team?"

"Not good, not bad, babe." JC Monroe greeted Percy with a kiss.

"Meaning?"

"Will y'all tell him this ain't no horsey meat. He cute tho. Want a Fresca to start shugga? Cool down that stiff neck you got." Katrina brushed her hair back.

"Sure. Can you put a double of Stoli in it?"

"Stoili?"

"What vodkas do you have?"

"Ohhhh, shurin nuff. We only have Uncle Benny's 3250th."

"Sure, whatever."

"Don't choo worry none. Benny makes the best vodkee in the state. Grows his own potaters and puts watermelon juice in the still. Made from right here in Lincoln."

"Just bring a double please. No Fresca. Just ice. That's all for now. I'll order food in a few. Thanks, uh, Katrina?" Percy strained to see her name tag.

"On the house handsome. Bet yer mama prolly told you that all the time. Handsome devil. Lawd, is it hot in here? Be rat back. Shoot. Need a Benny two times please, and one ice water for me!" She hollered to the bar as she walked away combing her hair with her fingers.

"Guess you got a local belly warming coming this evening boss." Yuri chuckled from his seat at the table.

"Shut up Yuri. Is this normal?" Percy sat with the team.

"Yea. You get use to it. This horsey thing is delish though. Need it in the city." Yuri scarfed down the last of his pony.

"Booker. Thank you for everything." Percy placed his hand on big Booker's shoulder.

"Awe mang we done fucked up. Shoulda been there at the cut when they got there but they pulled a quick one on us. We figured they be coming out the theater and go down the sidewalk the same way they come in. M'sorry bruh. But we gonna come correct with this shit even if it kills me. D is my heart. Fuck these crooked-ass racist cracker-ass-crackers and deez greasy ass mob fucks."

"Shhhh. Not so loud." JC placed a finger over her lips.

"Whateva. Mufukkas gonna pay. Copped me a chrome .44 snub just in case. Need my shotgun up dis mufukka mang. It's come down to this Perce. No bullshit. Ask JC and Yuri."

"So it's real? The Outfit is really here?"

"Yep. Frongello's in town. Tracked him inside the court house for over two and a half hours. Two-hundred percent more time needed to file a brief."

"And the perp, Smerkers. Darnell has excellent memory, down to the last pimple and tattoo on his arms. He's a real doozy this one. Barbara Sizemore gave me his file. A lost and nasty soul. Sherriff won't hear any of it. He's covering up also. Not sure why yet. More mystery figure out. But the answer is getting closer. I can feel it." JC flipped through some papers.

"Any idea where the kid is?"

"We working on it boss." Booker chomped on his tooth pick.

"Thanks Book. Hey, it's not on you. Me and JC didn't move fast enough or strong enough when we needed to. Fuckers blind sided us in the state house. But I ain't gonna worry about that now. We got some ground pounding ahead of us. You got the office set up?"

"Yes baby. We have the space in City Hall. Your brother used his Deputy Mayor status and got us the hook up. Barbara Sizemore paved the way for the tech and comms set ups. Multiple landlines, untraceable and traceable. Phone booth on the roof and…"

"Wai wai wait. A what?"

"Oh yea. The untraceable line is in a phone booth on the roof of City Hall. Crazy but perfect." JC grinned.

"Ok. Why in the name of… never mind. Horse meat and watermelon vodka for lunch, I'm not surprised. So you telling me I can call Chicago from the roof with a quarter?"

"Basically." Yuri shoved the last fry in his mouth.

"Wow. What else is new?"

"Oh there is something else," Yuri wiped ketchup from his mouth.

"Yea?"

"There's a broad conspiracy in town. Not sure who started it but we can guess. There's a collective effort to spread a big lie around town about Darnell's guilt. This will taint all potential jurors. Not uncommon in a small town like this. So we need to go unconventional on juror selection. It's in two days. There's been an all out effort launched at the VFW, barber shops, churches, bars, farms, factories, dealerships, ice cream parlors, hair salons, you name it." Yuri said wiping his mouth of white parmesan sauce.

"Damn. That figures bout right. I talked with Butch and Cannon before I came down. They have even more intel on land and zoning and permitting and development applications all over this area. They cover miles north to outside of Bloomington. West as far as Mason City. East as far as Clinton. South to Williamsville, and all the townships within that circle." Percy rummaged through his notes.

"Damn! Why?" JC asked.

"Exactly. This is big. I can't undertand how Darnell ties into it, but I have a sense that he does."

"How? Why?" Yuri mouthed behind a bottle of Orange Crush soda.

"Fuckin mob shit," Booker slapped the table.

"That's our job to find out more. But first we need to get Darnell out of this mess." Percy slapped the table back.

"The fellas are split up covering all corners of this area. If that little shit pops a pimple above ground, we will hear about it and bust his zit." Booker sucked his tooth pick.

"Can y'all cover all that?" Percy asked.

"We got reinforcements." Booker stared at him with fire in his eyes.

"Who? Never mind. I don't wanna know."

"Best you don't," Booker spit out his toothpick.

The defense team covered more details with Percy and showed him maps of the lay of the land in town and Central Illinois around Lincoln. They kept the most sensitive information off of the table, not to talk of those things in the restaurant accept for one vital piece of information.

"There is one thing I discovered you all need to know." A pensive Percy searched each one of their eyes.

- Lincoln Train Depot

- Blue Dog Inn

  https://www.enjoyillinois.com/explore/listing/blue-dog-inn/

Part 3

GAME ON

CHAPTER 10

RENDEZVOUS

Motel 7, across from the largest
covered wagon in the world

"Now, I'm craving your body
Is this real
Temperature's risin I don't wanna feel
I'm in the wrong place to be real
Whoa when I'm longing to love you
Just for a night
Kissin and huggin and holdin you tight
Please let me love you with all my might
Reasons
The reasons that we're here
The reasons that we fear
Our feeling's won't disappear
Oh, and after the love game has been played
All our illusions were just a parade
And all our reasons start to fade"

Knock knock on door 169.

Earth Wind and Fire's love ballad echoed from a portable cassette player on Desiree's hotel night stand. She sprayed wisps of Obsession by Calvin Klein on her neck and chest.

"So you are a gentleman." She unleashed her pearly whites.

"Of course. I open doors, pull out chairs and make sure I satisfy." Red pressed himself to control his crimson rush to his face with some effort.

"Oh my. Glad I'm dark as chocolate. Would hate for you to see me blushing. Is it hot in here?" Desiree stepped aside to let him in the room as she covered her face to perform a shy and blushing act.

"That purple dress is absolutely stunning. You look like a royal African queen. You remind me of my days of work in Namibia and the Congo."

"So worldly sir."

"Is that the Temptations I'm hearing?

"Oh and you know your music too. Love me a cultured man." She tuned away from him and rolled her eyes at his musical ignorance and to show her deep cut dress and exposed back.

"Is that Chanel I am noting?"

"And a keen olfactory sense as well? Hmmm. You do come as advertised." Two for two on the bullshit dummy meter.

"Good ads you display. I hope they are not the classifieds. Your pheromones are off the charts sweety. Are you okay?" McDougle searched her demeanor for distrust as she seemed a bit evasive.

He smirked as he strode into the room like he owned it. Feeling his opening argument was a winner, he began making his case as to why getting to third base on his first at bat is reasoning for his superstar status. Surveying the room with guarded suspicion, he looked for any sign of a trap. He moved through the little room conspicuously touching the drapes, lamps, telephone, looking for listening devices. A peek in the bathroom for a third party. He took the phone handset off of the receiver and placed a small couch pillow over it.

"Looking for something Red?"

"Just feeling the room. Don't want to be disturbed. Gives me pleasure that I connect with my environment before I…I mean we move our pieces around the board."

"I love it. But I'm not much of a gamester my dear. But I do like Red wine. Does this one meet your honor's approval?"

"How apropos. In my honor? How sweet. Pinot Noir. Perfect color."

"Red of course your Honor. Care to do the honors?" She smiled passing the bottle and cork screw to him.

"I know of a great little Mexican spot not far from here. Are you familiar with El Mazaltan? Best Mexican food between Springfield and Chicago, hands down."

"Sounds delish. Do they have hot tamales?"

Mcdougle laughed as Desiree peered at him through sultry eyes, ramping up her game.

"The best. You are a steamy chocolate fondue aren't you?"

"I just know what I want, when I it and how I need it."

"Let me change the music while you play bartender."

"Yes, I'll pop the cork."

"MMMMM, nice."

"I'm every woman, It's all in me
Anything you want done baby
I'll do it naturally
I'm every woman, It's all in me
I can read your thoughts right now
Every one from A to Z
I can cast a spell
With secrets you can tell
Mix a special brew
Put fire inside of you
Anytime you feel danger or fear
Instantly I will appear, cause
I'm every woman

Anything you want done baby
I'll do it naturally"

McDougle moved closer to her. She reached for his tie to loosen it. McDougle stared down at her big almond eyes, evaluating, percolating.

"I love that Aretha Franklin music."

"Um…Oh yes. Me too. She is really something. She says it good baby. Oh Red. *(such a moron, don't know ReeRee from Chaka)*"

"But I have requirements ya no." He teased.

"Like what?"

"This is not a meeting. This is an informal gathering amongst two superior masters of their crafts. Therefore you must help me get rid of this tie and unbutton my top button. If you behave I will help you unbutton the next button." He fingered a line down her bare shoulder.

Teasing the next button below, she dropped her head and eyes all the way down south. He looked down at her well groomed afro, feeling superior. Queen to rook.

"Well these are the type of meetings I prefer. Are we on for reservations? Is there a time we need to arrive? I hate to rush things. Slow and steady wins the race." She teased his clothing.

"Open seating, no hurry my dear. They know me. We will have the best seats and service whenever we arrive. Patron ritas on the rocks already on standby."

He popped the cork. She jumped and pulled away from him a bit.

"That was quick! I must be better than I give myself credit for." He smirked.

They both laughed as McDougle poured the red Pinot into hotel utility glasses.

"Is that blushing I see coming on you Red? My my, your nick name is the real deal. Ears, cheeks, neck, nose and… well, hmm. So cute. This wine is like a blood elixir. So hot. Let's toast."

"How about to connections, trust, transparency."

"And hot tamales?" She grinned at his eyes.

"Yes, and hot tamales."

Clink

"You know African queens have sex slaves." she kicked off her purple and gold Jo-Anne Vernay pumps.

"Eunuchs right?"

"Yessir. Built to serve their queen. Of course she only selects the best. Those proven masters in the art. Mmmm such a luscious back of palette warmth from this Pinot." She turned her back to him showing the deep cut lunge opening of the purple dress that reached just short of her ass cleavage. He reached around to her front, gently rubbing from top to bottom. She pulled away slowly towards the bed. Swiping her finger tips gently across the turned down sheets. She turned down the Chaka Khan volume.

"So as professionals, you think this case is open and shut?"

"Must we talk business now?"

"Well, I am here only for a short time. Gotta file something soon. My editor hounds me like every hour. Just want to know if I can get back to Chicago sooner than later. All this corn kind of creeps me out. Reminds me of that movie, Children of the Corn."

"Well let's just say I won't keep you lingering around our little podunk too long. Small towns don't usually have drawn out cases. I will see to it." He whispered in her ear.

"Such power you have here my big Reddy."

"It comes at a cost my dear." He rubbed his lips on her long chocolate neck down to her shoulder reveal. "But I love being able to chart my own destiny. These little hicks are a breeze.

You would be surprised how many cases I can get in and out of court quickly."

She broke away and refreshed his glass.

"Wow! Love me some power and control. Says a lot about a man's other life outside of work. How can a girl resist? You don't have a problem with the eunuch title do you?"

"I am a master of the art."

"A Picasso, Excellent."

They laughed again and toasted.

"That is a title I can live with if it comes with queen-like royal energy. Two powerful people knowing exactly what each one wants and how to get it. Now that's a nuclear explosion."

"Oh Red."

"Yes my queen?" He moved back into her. She broke the electricity again, moving to the window.

"My job is so stressful. I wish I could wrap this thing up quickly. The demands of the streets of Chicago keep me in an endless circus carousel of story after story after story. I work quick. I hate to linger. I'm not one of those Pulitzer seeking chicks trying to prove my womanhood amongst the men writers. I just want to tell it and get the fuck out. Stick and move, ya no?"

"I understand completely. I feel the same way. I hate being bogged down in lengthy trials. That's why I want this murder trial to go quickly. Once it gets to jury, I guarantee they will be in and out. Slam dunk. This thing is so obvious. That little nig…kid disappointed us all. I helped him come here and he re-pays me by killing my cousin and her husband! A fine white couple who wanted so much to have this little black…I mean, child. Damn. I really screwed this one up. I don't know how I can live with myself." He feigns distress seeking her sympathy.

"What do you mean baby?" She stroked his cheek helping him fuel his story.

"I thought this kid was perfect for my cousin. I made sure he got adopted in-spite of the anti-interracial adoption laws in the state and the nation. I personally made sure it got passed quickly. I got that kind of juice ya'no."

"Oh baby. Your power is so damn intoxicating." She gave him small standing hip thrusts.

"Easy now."

"Mmmm. Take it slow baby. How did you do it?" She moved closer inside of his personal space, nosing his ear.

"Let's just say I have friends in high and low places. Together, I was able to gather their collective influences to get the vote through the house and senate fast. They all had something to gain from this adoption and I promised them their spoils if they signed off on the bill."

"You mean business people?"

"Some. This thing went through every channel I could open. State, feds, the church, mob fucks, even up to the Vatican. I have them all in my pockets baby. They know who I am."

"Oh Big Red, Reddy Big. I'm boiling right now baby. See this Black steam coming out my ears. The Vatican? You my hero baby. Got dayum! So fukkin hot." She tongue flicked his neck.

"Oh yea. The Outfit put me on to them. They even came to me."

"The Outfit? Mmmm. Yess baby." Her chocolate cheek smashed his red face. She squeezed his ass.

"Yea, everybody got fingers in this kid, handed to them by me. Your big red eunuch. The kid is the center of it all. And now he screws the whole thing up? He gotta go. I will have to answer to all of this and re-tool."

"Re-tool? I like tools baby."

"Let's just say the kid was only the beginning."

"Beginning of what?"

"The new legacy baby. The new order in Illinois is about to commence."

She reached down past his belt buckle. He jumped a little. He reached behind her rubbing her bare back, pushing a fingers down her back cleavage. She kissed his neck to up the flow. Unbuttoning the rest of his shirt buttons, McDougle reached for his belt buckle.

"Let me unbuckle this belt for you baby. I don't want you to struggle with it. I wanna see the real red tool now baby." She unzipped his pants.

"Ah yes. The Red tool breaths, finally he's fee." He cocked his head back in anticipation of soothing satisfaction.

KNOCK KNOCK KNOCK

"What the fuck!"

"Who is it damnit!" She yelled.

KNOCK KNOCK KNOCK

"Dray its Dvan. Open up quick!"

"Who the fuck is that?" McDougle froze in mid erection.

"It's ok. It's only my photographer. Coming! Don't move baby." She cracked open the door poking her head out.

"What is it! I'm busy damnit!"

"Dray, it's the station. They calling me. Said they tried to call your room but the phone is always busy."

"About what?"

"They said your father has been calling the station. Your mother had a heart attack and was rushed to the hospital. You need to call him now!"

"Oh my God! Ok. Ok. I'll call. Shit, shit, not now! Damnit!"

"I have your father on the phone now in my room. C'mon! Quick!"

She flung the door open wide and ran down the hall. Red stood frozen as a statue, shirt open, pants to his knees, his boxer shorts opening displayed his saluting Sir Redness sticking out. Dvan's eyes locked on McDougle's, then drifted down to the boxers. Say hello to my little red friend. They both froze.

"I'll be right back Red ok?" She called from the hallway running.

"Hey guys I'm really sorry. I, I, I didn't mean to break up your party. I didn't know."

"No party here damnit!" Pulling up his pants, he slammed the door shut.

- Largest covered wagon in the world sits just outside of the Hotel Lincoln Inn

  https://destinationlogancountyil.com/world-s-largest-covered-wagon

CHAPTER 11

REESE 2.0

Just South of Lincoln Lakes, Railsplitter Park was recently renamed Edward R. Madigan Park State Fish and Wildlife Area. Done to honor the Lincoln born businessman, Lincoln College graduate, and Republican Party politician, who served in the House of Representatives from 1967-1973.

The 975 acre fish and wildlife area along the Salt creek, is a sanctuary destination for Lincolnites to enjoy fishing, biking, canoeing, wildlife, native bird watching, picnicking and deer hunting. The dense forest habitat is home to a lush canopy of walnut, oak, ash, hickory, and the largest sycamore tree in Illinois, towering over 350 feet.

Local explorers enjoy burrowing deep within the park sprinkled with outdoor stoves, shelters, toilets, cabanas, drinking water and playground equipment. An easy maze to get lost in or hide out for long periods.

On the eastern edge of the park, is a 50-acre farm surrounded by a heavily treed housing compound. The mini-maze of housing structures, sheds, small barns, deep water wells and maintenance garages back up to the park.

In the distance, barreling down on 12225th street, an approaching dust cloud kicked up gravel behind a Lincoln Town Taxi Service 1965 Ford Galaxy 500. Coming to a dusty stop at the entrance to the compound, not a soul can be seen.

"Is this it?" Booker asked peering through the front and side windows of the taxi.

"Yea. That'll be six bucks. Hurry please. I don't like being down these parts, especially at twilight." The cab driver nervously extended his hand for the cash.

"Why not?" Asked Chick.

"Just some weird things be going on down around here I heard." The cabby did a 360 look-around of the compound entrance.

"Like what?" Booker also looked around.

"I don't know. Town folk have all kinds of stories about weird sounds coming outta here. People say it's the home of some kind of voodoo mojo tribe. I don't fuck around with it. Y'all sure you spose to be here?"

"This the address right?" Jimmy barked irritated.

"Yea boss. This it. Can I get that six bucks now? I got kids."

"Here ya go. Thanks" Booker pushed the cash in his hand.

"Good luck." The driver hurried them out of the cab.

"Damn. What's his problem?" Jimmy adjusted his sunglasses looking around more.

"Local bullshit. HELLO! ANYBODY HERE?" Booker called out.

"Maybe they went to the store." Chick turned circles looking for any movement.

Bird chirps suddenly stopped.

"The fuck?"

"Shhhh. Listen."

"I don't hear nuthin."

"Egggactly." Booker looked up and around suspiciously.

"Hello!" We looking for Reese!" Booker called to the air.

Silence

"Mee Zeh" (Who is it?) A call Hebrew came from the trees.

"Eh-khad she khoht-tseh Nah-har (The one who crosses the river)" Booker responded.

"Mee whoo-Eh-loh-hem (Why is God?)." The response back to him.

"Lih-khah-sote eem dham (To cover with blood)" Booker retorted.

In a sudden roar, the deep plum GTO Judge bolted at them screaming from the tree thicket. Smoke, sand, gravel and thousands of tree leaves flew wildly around the car. It raced directly toward the fellas. Its front end rose off the ground like it blasted from the starting line at a street drag race.

As fast as it charged at them, it dove to a sliding dirt digging stop in front of them. The fellas held fast as the dragon came to a hissing shut down. The driver door opened.

"Good to see ya fellas. She's precision tuned now. Don't know who was working on her before, but Ms. Sheeba is fine now. It's like somebody gave her a back alley abortion then put a band-aid on her to stop the bleeding. But she ready now. Oh, and is she ready." Darryl Reese approached them smiling a gap-tooth grin.

"The hell you mean? Your brother put that thing together and we did some tweaking. What the hell did you do to her?" Jimmy shot back walking around the sparkling deep plum beast.

"No wonder. No worries. What ever she's confronted with now, my baby girl will rain hell fire down on it. Got her up to 625 horse power. Suspension much firmer to handle whatever she run-up on. Bored out the chambers. Upped the piston size of course. Much bigger diameter from the heads to the tail pipes. More cold air in and out. She racing specs now baby! Y'all headin to the track to get paid?"

"Naw. We got work and no time to waist. What is all this down here? And why did I have to say all that crazy shit coming in here?" Booker asked looking around the compound.

"Bro. You know where you at right now?"

"If I did I wouldn't ask."

"Man this is Home Shalom."

"Sha-what?" Booker's face twisted in question.

"You in the presence of God now. My brothers of the African Israelites run this mutha. You on sacred grounds."

"What you talking about?" Jimmy stepped forward.

"Man this is ground zero for the Black Sayeret Matkal." Reese waved his arms around like introducing the world.

"This is what Butch had tole me about. Thought he was trippin." Booker said between his toothpick-clutching teeth.

"The baddest brothers in the state. Motherland truth boy." Darryl grinned.

"Man, what are you taking about?" Chick asked.

"You heard of the African Israelites from back home?"

"Yea. Them African wanna-be back to Africa dudes?" Chick continued to look around for more movements.

"Naw son, they the truth. They connected to ancient Israel and the original Black African slaves of Egypt. I'm talkin Moses, son. I'm talking Enoch boy! Betta recognize." Reese was more serious now.

"Say what? Man what this dude sayin?" Jimmy asked."

"Yup. And they are versed in the ancient ways of worship, society, culture, and war. This group here is the Divine War Mid-Western Faction. This is the U.S. training grounds for the greatest war fighters on the planet. I'm tellin you, this is the real deal. And by you saying those words, you just saved your necks coming up in here. But I told them you were coming."

"So you one of them?" Booker asked.

"Sort of. They kind of adopted me to take care of all things mechanical. In turn, they hook me up with my wives, and a home and ..."

"Wai wait. Your wives?" Chick perked up in wonder.

"Oh yea. I have three wives. And they all fine-ass sistas from back home.

We have six children and they all brilliant. We discovered true love and understanding. This how a real family works out here baby! Community, family, empathy, joy, work and care for others. Use our God given abilities to raise children and create peace and love and family strength, peace, harmony and security."

"Hmmm" Chick not sure what to say.

"Now this is generational wealth son. Safety and security. Health and peace. But we don't take no shit off them peckerwoods. These boys are the most sophisticated fighters and killers in the world son, no joke."

"Bobby be got -dayum!" Booker scratched his head.

"Oh yea. And we all physically fit…the women, kids, elders. We all work-out daily. Stay off the meat. No smoking, no drinking and all that stuff. We clear son. Verrrrry clear out here. Fresh food we grow in the best soil in this jacked up country. We can have it all, if we can handle it. If not, no problem, you can just bounce. But we must keep certain oaths. I don't see everything the brothers do, only the family stuff. This place is like what heaven spose to be, dig?"

"Ummmmm ok. Your brother Ernie know about all this?" Jimmy looked at Reese side-ways.

"Sort of but not really. He wouldn't understand. He caught up in the street life still. I get it. I was in it too. No biggie. We talk all the time. We good. Wanna look around?"

"We don't have much time. Maybe later." Booker took the keys from Darryl and started to head to the car.

"Cool. I'll introduce you to someone before ya'll split."

Darryl whistled an odd whistle and a man appeared from the front of a wide oak tree. He blended into the bark and was not seen when they were dropped off.

Carrying an oak staff and wearing a robe that looked like tree bark, he spoke with clarity and purpose.

"My brothers. I am Ben Israel Al Shafari. How are you? Good to see you can retrieve your fine car from our master mechanic," he extended both hands shaking all with a firm grip and a piercing hazel-eyed stare.

"Yea, good to meet you. What you got going here?" Booker asked with an air of suspicion.

"Ha! As Brother Darryl said, this is our home where we live and train and study. We are fully self-sustaining, no county utilities. We generate our own power, water and food. We have about a total of 55 acres around the area and several other large patches in other strategic areas of the state."

"Strategic?" Booker asked with a raised eyebrow.

"Yes. We planted ourselves here not only to sustain life but to also monitor life. We are staged in various areas strictly as a means to protect ourselves from any harm or other nonsense that may arise. We understand that we do not fit the mold around here and we know how things can get when locals see something they don't understand. Your country is full of hate, division, fear, and hypocrisy. There is no true religion here. This is no secret. It's your history. So we established our community here with these fundamental understandings and are ready for pretty much anything they throw at us, from the farm to the courtroom. We were all born in this country so we are very clear on how the system operates."

"So y'all don't work?" Jimmy asked.

"Of course we work. Our men have jobs around the era. We blend in with them. We teach and attend the Universities around here. Most of our men have Masters and PhD.s The women mostly have 2 or 4 year degrees then focus on home and children, home-schooling them. Once the kids are grown, the women take on other, let's say, strategic roles."

"How many y'all down here and why here?

"Ha! Well, we have about 350 in the Central Illinois area. We came here from Chicago about 10 years ago. First it was for the agriculture and clean living. Can't raise children in Chicago, certain death. We initially focused on various crops, some new, some experimental, some foreign, like the Neem tree. Once word got out and we started earning substantial income from the Neem plant, more came, we expanded. But we knew we had to also defend our lifestyle."

"So y'all like black hippies?" Chick giggled.

"Not at all. We are God focused and driven. No getting high and tuning out.

We are driven to build our human capital and cash reserves and then make the move off content back home to Israel, to a little town called Damona. We have a thirty-year plan."

"What you mean defend your selves?" Booker looked around for any surprises.

"Our soldier forces train in the ways of the Sayeret Matkal."

"Ok. There's that word again," Jimmy injected stepping forward.

"Yes. Sayeret Matkal is like your American Army Delta Force, Seals, and Para Rescue, all in one. It's an Israeli field intelligence gathering unit. But also a deep recon team, as well as a counter-terrorism and hostage rescue unit. It is extremely top secret but we have members here who were part of the force in Israel who train our brothers. Now Israelis come here two or three times a year to give us up to date trainings and learn our specific tactics in the States. It has been considered the most difficult combat training in the world."

"How so?" Jimmy asked.

"We go through a twelve-month infantry training, including paratroop training. Twelve weeks of counter-terror warfare training. We do long range reconnaissance patrols of 100-miles in one week. Trainees are held captive as prisoners for three weeks and forced to perform realistic demeaning tasks. Of course there are various small arms, hand combat and other weapons training."

"Y'all got guns here?" Booker snapped.

"We have guns at many locations," he smiled.

"Hmm."

"As well, they all must attain undergraduate degrees in various intelligence, political, computer, chemical and natural sciences, health care and other degree plans."

"Damn. And they are here, now?" Jimmy looked around.

"Oh yea, but you will never know it," Ben Israel giggled.

"Cool." Chick holding his toothpick in his teeth.

"Well, it is great meeting you brothers. I hope you find what you are looking for. I must tend to some things here. Feel free to stay and eat.

Darryl can show you around the compound."

"I wanna know where I can get me three or four of those fine sistas," Chick giggled.

"Well you can. If you are willing to come into our community. A great and wonderful commitment. We would love to have you."

"Welllll." Chick back peddled.

"Yea. It took me a minute to join. I couldn't get off those Newports, pig feet and Schlitz Malt Liquor Bulls." Darryl laughed.

"Yes, we do have rules. And those are definite no-nos. Hope to hear from you. But there are great troubles in town now. We are monitoring," Said Ben Israel.

A sudden whoosh of air startled a flock of birds from a large oak tree behind them. The fellas turned quickly, nervously to see what the noise and action was. They gazed in wonder at the birds taking flight. When they turned back around, Ben Israel was gone. They looked around for him as he seemed to have vanished into thin air.

"We gotta get moving. You heard about the shootings?" Booker asked Darryl.

"Yep. On it. Nothing gets past us. It's what we do. Take care of the little Dragon Princess, ok? She has some new cool features added you will discover. Test them out before you need them."

"She's in good hands bro. Thanks for everything. And take care of those babies," Jimmy added.

"And them sistas!" Chick smiled climbing into the Judge.

"Oh you know it. Be careful out there. And check your six at all times," Darryl waved them off.

"What he mean by that?" Chick looked at Booker and Jimmy.

"Hell if I know," Booker responded from the back seat.

"It means watch your ass." Jimmy injected from behind the wheel.

"Damn. I thought he meant check our six pack of Bull." Chick giggled.

"Shut up fool! Jimmy scoffed as he gingerly guided the new and improved Dragon GTO Judge down the 12225th Street dirt road en-route to Atlanta to start the hunt for Russell.

- Edward R. Madigan Park State Fish and Wildlife Area (https://dnr.illinois.gov/parks/park.edwardrmadigan.html)

CHAPTER 12

THE RIVER

"Are you in or you out? I ain't got all night. I'm all in baby, oh yea!"

Deacon pushed all of his cash of three hundred and fifty dollars into the pot hoping the table didn't call his bluff.

"You bitches know I don't bluff so you better get your holy booty's out while the getting is good cuz you know the Deac is holdin them royals. Or is the Deacon bluffin? Ha! You ain't neva know. What? What? Ha ha!! C'mom bitches! Let's go! The Deac is rollin tonight!"

The remaining five players around the table fidgeted, wiping their brows, and looked at each other unsure. Knowing he has bluffed them before but he is now holding high cards. There's more than five-hundred dollars cash in the pot. Each player is down to their last twenty or thirty dollars. Deacon sucked his teeth, chewed on a toothpick, tried to play it cool. His leg nervously bounced like a jack hammer underneath the table. A ten, Jack, and Queen of spades showed on the Texas Hold'em river. The threat of Deacon showing an Ace and King of spades scared the table.

"Hey Big Mike, can I get two-hundred on credit to put in now? I'm trying to go to Vegas next week baby!" Deac raised the fear higher. "C'mon niggas! I got a fee-let mig-non I'm tryna catch up with at that little Frenchy wee-wee spot in Springfield. Does anyone know the best year for a Pinot New-wha to pair with a medium rare, a little bloody on the inside?

Ha haaa! Gonna get those scalloped potatoes and them white asparagus veggies to round out the plate. MMMMMMM. Maybe get them mussels in wine garlic sauce to start after I bust y'alls nuts wide open! LET'S GO YALL!!! I got a piece of chicken waitin on me at the motel. Ya'll country-ass bammas so damn slow! Pissin me off. Let's git it! Put up or shut up!"

Deacon talked more shit, baiting the table to put in or fold. After four rounds of betting and a swollen pot of more than 700 dollars, everyone folded.

"Well la-di-da. The Deac's goin out tonight baby! Oh yea!" Deacon grabbed the money pot and stood up.

"Thank you my sheep. I'm loanin cash at fifty cent on the dollar on your money. Any takers? Hurry up. My chicken callin me like a tweety bird. Tik Tok y'all. Clock tickin. 3-2-1. Sheeeeiiiiiit. I'm gittin up outta here."

"Hold on! Let's see your cards Deac!" A player demanded from across the table.

"Ain't my problem."

Deac got up sorting the cash. Stuffing the wad in his shirt pocket. He quickly flipped his cards over revealing mis-matched low numbers. Not one spade or royal in his hand. The table erupted with anger.

"Ain't nobody tell you to play this silly-ass Texas grab ass game. Be glad I ain't take your car keys or your women. I'm out." Deacon quickly exited the play area amidst the complaining and angry gaggle around the table.

"Hey Deak, can I talk to you for a minute?" A concerned Pastor Greenwood signaled him over.

"Of course pastor. Wus on your mind?"

"You heard the horrible news in Lincoln? About the Wagner's?"

"Yes. This has me truly distressed. I must confess something to you Pastor."

"What's troubling you?"

"Ya see, that boy, Darnell. I know him from back in the city. And well, I'm really here to keep an eye on him and report back his situation, and now this."

"Oh I see now. I thought there was something a little off about you."

"What you sayin!?"

"I mean in a good way. You seemed a little distracted and were asking me some pointed and odd questions about the Wagners' and other things. Now it makes sense."

"Please forgive me pastor. I'm just looking out for his interest. I know his father."

"Do you think he killed his adopted parents?"

"HELL NO! Oh, my bad. Of course not."

"Neither do I. Matter of fact, the only person crazy enough to do something like that is the mob or that crazy juvie white boy."

"Who?"

"That Russell kid. Lives out in East Lincoln, off Limit Street out near the Knights of Columbus. I think his mama works at the Precision factory out there. He's done all kinds of horrible things around town for years. Even up here in Atlanta. Stole things. Gets in fights. He even stole a cop car."

"Say what?"

"Yea. Something telling me he knows something."

"Something?"

"You hear about Jay at Kroger?"

"Who?"

"The guy who got hurt by Russell when he stole some rib-eyes steaks?"

"Umm. Now this some real country-ass bamma shit. Oops. Sorry Pastor."

"Never mind. But actually the day of the Wagner murders, Spunk Lee told me he saw him running out of the alley behind the theater. Spunk was back there doing trash pick up with his sanitation truck when the kid ran in front of his truck without looking. Spunk almost hit him. Said he was limping bad but still running in a panic. Dragging his leg. He flipped Spunk the bird as he limped away."

"What he look like?"

"Ole dirty white boy. I think he's about five foot nine, a hundred forty pounds drenched. Skinny. Dirty redish hair. Pimply ugly face.

"Why you think he may be involved?"

"Just a feeling. It's weird how all these horrible things happening around here lately started after the rib-eyes was stolen. The horrible fires and all. Everything was running fine until all that stuff happened recently."

"Thank you pastor. I will let my team know about this."

"Is this helpful information?"

"It is. Big time stuff. Thank you."

"Well I tell you what. Sense I helped you, maybe you can help me?"

"Anything, name it. But I don't do rib-eyes."

"Ha! Well this is Tips and Tithes night ya'no. And you just cleaned out the kitty. Those brothers give fifty percent of their winnings to the church. How about you go back in there and, let's say you loose a few hands, maybe more than a few. Good info ain't cheap."

"Uh huh."

"Ya no. Get the brothers their money back. The more you loose, the more the church gains, the more information I may have for you."

"Ain't this a bitch. You just played me like a two-dollar hoe. Ok Pastor Slick. Maybe you should be the new Sneakin Deacon of Lincoln."

"No it's not like that."

"I gotchoo. Damn you good. That was some gangsta shit right there. I feel ya. I was gonna buy this little Asian thing dinner tonight. Least I can do since she out of a job at the Tropics Lounge since it burned down. Damn! Come to think of it. I think I saw that pimply little twit you talking about at the Tropics the night of the fire. Son of a…"

"The lord will truly bless you my brother."

"Yea yea. Damn. Almost had me a nut."

Deac returned to the poker table.

"Who wants another crack at ch'alls money? Interest free bitches. I'm feeling generous tonight."

The players hoot it up and sit back down to play.

"Seven cards, nothing wild. Down and dirty. Get back to black game'in up in this mutha mangk! A real game not that cowboy shit. If you was my hoes, I'd been slapped the mascara off all y'all. I'm dealing. Let's git it!"

Deacon turned on the charm like a light switch. The players giggled at his silliness. Grateful for another chance at their money.

- Down and dirty

CHAPTER 13

SPITTIN

Deep in the corn fields, a few miles east of Lincoln, the small town of Beason, population 120, is where Russell had been living out of the Mob's black Lincoln, nursing his busted knee. The locals began staring at the double black Lincoln tucked behind a corn shed. Won't be long before someone comes knocking on the window. Low on fuel, and money, he limped the car north on Logan County 6. Crossing the Kickapoo creek, hoping to park it at the Hickory Lane Campground. He arrived at the entrance, the gate was locked.

Easing the Linc slowly north, saving what little gas was left in the tank, he crept the car up 2100th Ave, another of the dirt roads connecting endless acres of winter corn. The road soon split into 2350th Avenue, more dirt bisecting more corn. He didn't realize the split turned him back west close to the I-55 interstate, just outside of the town of Atlanta. That's where the Linc spit its last sputter.

Guiding it slowly off of 2350th into a tractor path buried in corn rows, he gathered up his few things and started limping towards the small historic town of Atlanta. He knew he could not go back to Lincoln. Everyone was looking for him.

Hobbling along 2350th Avenue looking over his shoulder at every step, he tried to keep a low profile. The avenue became E. South St. He painfully walked his way under the I-55 interchange crossing Rt. 66 into the heart of Atlanta. He considered going into Roady's Atlanta Travel Center

Truck Stop, but reconsidered after seeing a gaggle of truckers hanging around at the busy stop.

Not wanting to be seen, he kept moving towards town on SW Arch St. The police station to his left, he quickly turned right. He found himself at the feet of a 30 foot tall Paul Bunyan statue holding a massive hot dog. Looking up, he salivated at the big dog-man's steamy massive meat. He saw Missy's Sweet Shop directly across the street. He went inside Missy's hoping no people were in there. Tourists are ok, they will be moving on. He saw all kinds of yummy treats and cakes. Smells of freshly baked cookies and homemade ice creams ramped up his hunger more.

More odd grumbling and wheezing sounds from his stomach began to hurt now. Down to his last four dollars, two of those in quarters. He must make good cheap choices for food or get more money. He eyed the hot cinnamon buns Missy brought out with fresh snicker doodle cookies, filling the air with a hot cinnamon bouquet. His dry mouth watered. He heard a bell ding behind him. A black guy was playing a one-ball machine. A pin-ball game that pays cash. But a quarter only gives one ball to possibly win twenty dollars. The black guy went outside seemingly happy that he just hit for cash. Russell dug out one of his last quarters from his pocket to test his luck. He pulled the lever. The ball missed the twenty dollar payoff by one slot space. He fumed loudly. Cursing. He saw Missy serving the same black guy a steamy gooey double cheeseburger and fries. He dropped another quarter. So close again, and again. Getting louder with frustrated demoralized anger, he pounded the machine. Down to his last quarter. No luck. He cursed then pounded the machine. Startled patrons watched him storm out of Missy's.

He avoided the police station and headed down S.E. Race St. The Red Wing Bowling Alley could be a stop. Maybe get a job cleaning for food. Pulling on the door, it was locked. A handwritten sign read, *"Sorry Hookers We Closed Fer HVAC Repairs - No 7-10s Today - Keep on Hookin - Back Monday my lovely ballers"*

He needed to rest his leg and think. A mild winter chill in the air yet he felt hot sun beams cooking him. His temperature rose and his head hurt from dehydration. He saw the J.H. Hawes Grain Elevator Museum next to the bowling alley. A fully restored red wooden grain elevator built in 1904, now a tourist attraction. Fortunately no tourists were there. He went inside and stowed his things. He rested, was starving and thinking how to get food when he heard voices nearby. He eased out from the red wooden shelter of the Hawes elevator into the light. A line of black people formed on the street behind him. They were waiting to go into the Atlanta United Methodist Church. As he turned to go back inside, he heard his name called out.

"Russell? Hey Russell? Is that you man? Wus up?"

He quickly ducked back inside the grain elevator. He peeked out to see who was calling him. Worried it was a mob greaser or cop.

"Hey Russ is that you? It's me Stanley. What'chu doing in there man?"

Stanley Greenwood, Blue Dog Inn busboy and one of Pastor Stan's twin sons, came over to him with a smile wanting to see him.

"Hey man it's me Stanley, from school."

"Oh hey, wus up bro?"

"Man I ain't seen you in a minute. Damn. Since like 11th grade."

"Oh yea. Cool right."

"What you doing up here in Atlanta?"

"Just hangin out."

Stanley looked around seeing his cloths and few belongings. He noticed Russell looked disheveled, in pain, and worried.

"I'm up here going to my church. Wanna come? We got dinner and stuff going on now."

"Umm, umm, I ain't no church goer ya no?"

"It's not like that. We just come here to hang out, eat, chill. Lots of young people from all around. It's kinda our spot. They be playing cards and games and music and stuff. No church stuff today. C'mon. I'll introduce you to some of my boys."

"Y'all got food?"

"Oh yea plenty! And beer if you drink. I don't drink but its cool."

"Umm. Ok sure. I mean you sure its ok for me to go in there?"

"Oh. Yea. Everybody cool. Even some Puerto Rican dudes and one dude who dresses like a woman. But it's all good. No judging in there. That's why I come. It's a Jesus thing, ya'no? All welcome bro."

Inside the bustling and loud church basement meeting hall, Stanley saw that Russell was not comfortable. He got food for him and they sat away from the people. He could tell Russell was in pain and running from something. They both dropped out of high school about the same time. Stanley, because of a new baby with his girlfriend, and Russell for getting locked up. Stanley knew Russell's reputation for being stupid and reckless.

"So how long you been coming here?" Russell asked between slurps of chicken dumpling soup and spoons of mac-n-cheese.

"Been here for several years." Stanley said.

"Guessin you like this?"

"Oh yea. Especially since I can get away from stuff and hang here with no issues. Everybody here got stuff on their heads, ya no?"

"Yea? Like what?" Russell was more curious now.

"Stuff, ya'no? But I like it cuz I get to play music in the band."

"Ain't your pappy a priest or something?"

"Yea, he's the pastor here. But he don't force me to come. I come cuz I like it now. I didn't like it before. But now I'm older, I dig it, ya no?"

"Yea. Any more of those biscuits?"

"Sure, plenty."

Stanley gave him more biscuits and dumplings as Russell looked around at all the activity, suspicious and nervous.

"They playing cards for money over there?"

"Yea. Them dudes always gamblin. Cards, craps, roulette." Stanley grinned proud.

"Damn! Really?"

"Yup. Half of the money goes to the church. Hey, you wanna see my music studio here?"

"Uh I don't know."

"I got a few bong hits left. Grab a few beers, c'mon! It's in a separate part of the church. Can't smell the weed from out there."

"Uh, ok sure."

"I'll grab a two six packs from the cooler. You like Schlitz Malt Liquor Bull?"

"I guess. Never had it."

"It's got a kick."

"Cool."

In the music studio, Stanley set up bong hits. Russell slammed beers like it was his last day on earth. Stanley started playing his Fender Rhodes piano.

"Man you good at that shit."

"I try. Been playing my whole life. It's easy now."

"You like a pro or what? You on the radio and shit? Got records?"

"Naw man. Not like that, but I got a few recordings I'm working on. I always record my stuff. I even wrote a few songs with lyrics. You wanna hear some?"

"Sure. What's lyrics?."

Stanley turned on the cassette recorder and started signing and playing.

"Man that was cool. How you come up with them words and stuff?"

"I just sing about life. It's easy when you got something to say. You can do it. Wanna try?"

"Naw." Russell took another bong hit and polished off another 16 oz. Bull, then cracked open another.

"C'mon man. Just think about important stuff or hurtful stuff or funny stuff or serious stuff. Just say what you feel. Man I know you been through some crap, I remember back in the day. You probably got great songs in you. Maybe you can do country style. Wanna try?"

"Hell I don't know. Fuck. Shit. Ok. Like what?" He pulled another long swig of Bull, finishing the can. Then he reached for another and the microphone.

"I mean whatever you know about? What do you like or don't like?"

"Man, I know about cops and shit." He shotgunned the rest of the Bull and feeling more confident.

"Ok, I'll start playing piano with something cool like a cop show."

"But I can't sing."

"Don't sing, just say it. Rap it like Sugar Hill Gang."

"Who?"

"I'll blend the piano with whatever you do. Russell, believe you can do it man and you can do it. You Russell Smerkers man. I've seen you in action man. You can do it. Ready? Just get close to the mic and let it rip bro."

Stanley adjusted the recorder input volume.

Russell grabbed the mic beginning his weed and Schlitz Malt Liquor Bull fueled rap:

"I hate cops.
They suck ass.
They get in my way
when I'm being jazz
Stole me a car
they want it back
I crashed that fucker
I ain't given jack
They think they smarter than me
I can run and hide
I'm too slick for them
cuz I gotta get mine."

"Yea! Cool man. Keep going!" Stanley smiled and dug in deeper with his Fender Rhodes playing.

Russell poured some of his beer in the bong a sucked another long bong hit and another long Bull pull.

"I ain't scared of them or the mob
I get rid of people that blow my job
Burn down daycares or blow up a house
Hell I ain't no little scared mouse
They see me when I'm cookin
I get rid of them then I'm bookin.
I shoot him pop pop in his face
You won't find me any day
You squeal on me I shoot you in the face
Moms and pops in the alley no chase
I bury chicks under the road
and burn Tropics to the ground
That's how I get down

You see me steal steaks
I make you pay
I'm the man cuz I goth them all today
They think I'm dumb
I cap them for fun
You cross me then you done
Redrum Redrum Redrum
It's the color that I done
Now I do it for fun
If you see me you better run
See me in the mirror
Redrum Redrum Redrum."

Stanley stopped playing. Trying to soften the stunned look on his face.

"What you think? You like it?" Russell smiled with pride.

"Uh, um, man! That's some dope cool stuff. You see. You can do songs. Man you should make a record on that. It would sell!"

"Maaaan, you think so? That felt good. I'll call it Redrum. You got any more weed?"

"Uh, yea. Knock it out man. Them some powerful lyrics."

"What's lyrics?'

"Ya no, the words. They felt so real."

"They are real. I live that shit cuz I'm a mobster."

"What you mean?"

"Don't say nothin, but they brought me in."

"Who?"

"The mob. They hear ya no? Watchin that nigger boy. But they tried to off me so I capped one of'em in the face and took his car. They lookin for me now."

"Why?"

"That's what I'm sayin! Why they wanna off me? I did what they asked me to do! I took out all the witnesses who saw me at Kroger! I proved myself like they asked me! Torched the house and the daycare and buried that bitch at that stupid Tropics bar. Fuck, we even burned it down! Ha! They know I am the real deal. Now they wanna cap me! ME! Well I showed them who's the real mobster. I took one of 'em out, now they looking for me. That's why I gotta keep movin. Man I need some money."

"Ummm, well I ain't got that. But maybe you can win at the card tables inside. Wanna try? You can get some credit. I'll cover for you but only for ten bucks."

"Naw. I need to get outta here."

Stanley stopped the recorder.

- Blood Music

CHAPTER 14

MUSCLE HEADS

Coon Hound Johnny's

With AJ dead and Russell on the run, Tony's hand was shaking like a windy leaf. His staccato slurps on bouncing spoons of chicken gnocchi soup made weird sounds. He knew Don Anaganino would be calling soon to see if the job of getting rid of Russell is done. He hasn't heard anything from the Don in days and that's not good. But he wasn't going to call him either with the bad news. Tony has been hole up at Coon Hound's ever since AJ got popped. Coon Hound disposed of AJ's body deep in the cornfields behind the tavern.

"Relax Tony. Have a couple more of these pink pills. They seem to keep you calm."

"I don't want another one of your fuckin tabs Johnny! I'm sweatin bullets here! No word. Questo silenzio della morte." (The silence of death)

"Maybe you should call him?"

"Are you insane Johnny? Jeezus fuck me will'ya!"

"You want Malina to take you in the back and work things out of you?"

"FOR GODS SAKE JOHNNY! I ain't thinkin bout no kitty poon tang right now. OKAY!!"

"Jus tryna help, thas'all."

RIIINNNGG!!

"FUCK!!" Tony jumped out of his chair. Chicken gnocchi soup juice splashed up and down on the table.

"Hello? Hey Jerry wus up? Yea. Ok. When? Yea. Ok thanks. Bye."

"Who's that?" Tony's eyes wide as a 12" pizza.

"Jerry Ogden, he owns the Bloody Bucket up the road. Said two muscles came in his joint lookin for AJ. Said they were just at the Lomax Café, then The Maple Club, and at The Black Tavern."

"Oh shit. That means they……

BOOOM!!!

The heavy wooden barn-style front doors with the bullet holes banged open. Two muscle-heads from the Outfit stormed in.

"Hey, which one of you is Coon Hound?"

"That's me."

"You seen AJ?"

"Who?"

"Don't fuckin jank me! You know got-damned well who I'm tawkin'bout. Where is he!?"

"He's gone."

"Who the fuck are you?"

"Tony."

"Ohhhh, so you the brains of this cluster fuck down here."

"Well, I'm just…"

"Just shut yer fuckin hole! Where's AJ and that kid? Show me the kid's grave."

"I can't."

"And why the fuck not?"

"Cuz the kid is gone and AJ is dead."

"Fuck you say?"

"The kid shot AJ and stole the car."

"Wait, what? The Don's kid is dead you say?"

"Yea."

"Do you have any idea what's going on in town?"

"Well, like what exactly?"

"You livin under a rock out here or wha? You smell like horse shit."

"Basically."

"Shut up! The nigger kid. You know about his parents?"

"Yea, what about'em? We been tailing'em every day, well at least until AJ got shot."

"And you doing a bang up job of it Captain America. But you're done here."

"What?"

"We yooz replacements."

Tony's body stiffened like paste.

"Are you Clank and Doni?"

The two goons looked at each other roaring in sadistic laughter.

"Wha, wha, what's so funny?"

"Clank and Doni Boy are now Mud Man and Dirt Boy. They be hangin with Aquaman in the Chicago River. Suppose they a couple of fuckin mermaids bout now. BA HA HAAAA!!" The two sadistics' couldn't contain their gut laugh. Tony swallowed hard.

"Hey Coonhound, where's yer phone?"

"Right here sir."

"You got any riga?"

"Yes. Two bowls coming up. Malina!! Two bowls riga, now!"

"Just need one."

One goon dialed the phone, the other stared down Tony and Johnny like a red tailed hawk locked on a rabbit. Malina eased out of the kitchen with one bowl on a tray. Her long flowing jet-black Italian hair draped her full bra-less breasts under her half buttoned white silk blouse. Tight lips and nervous eyes painted now. She knew the drill of how to tone down a situation when heat came in smokin. Her required duty, just as she was taught back in Palermo. The goon held his stare on Tony, not blinking as Malina's strong scent of sandalwood and garlic wafted by him. Tony and Johnny locked in place while the other goon talked to the Don.

"Ok boss. Understand." He hung up the phone.
"Boss says you fucked up and you gotta go."
"But.....
POW POW POW POW!!!
Two shots from each goon's .45 plugged Tony. Two to the body, two to the head. Malina screamed, then fainted. Johnny put his hands up.
"Boss says you know what to do with this kinda mess, right?"
Johnny shook his head yes. The goons bounded out of Coon Hound Johnny's Tavern into their bronze 1976 Chrysler Imperial Le Baron. They headed south on Route 121.
Johnny tried to revive Melina.

CHAPTER 15

TWO OPTIONS

L ine one sir. It's 10am. Your Vatican call."

"I can tell time Chucky geez. Just cuz youza Hungarian don't mean youz know every friggin thing."

Chuck Csavossy, Don Niccolo Anaganino's executive assistant, understood his bosses angst, nothing personal. His own future could be on the line with this call.

"Good day my grace."

"Is it? So optimistic from such a grand leader. Optimism may be your down fall my good man. Don Niccolo."

Listening

"Sometimes unexpected occurrences can yield great rewards."

"Do I sense a spirit of optimism from the Vatican?" Don Niccolo asked.

"Like you Americans say, let's not get it twisted. At this point you have two options my dear Don Niccolo. Live or die."

Listening. Swallowing lumpy.

"As we have concluded here, your time has expired. Time to, how you say, stop fucking around. We need the following from you ASAP. One. We need you to find that fucking crazy kid and incinerate him. And two, you need to get this fucking train back on track and get these contracts operational statewide immediately. We are done janking your little pasta noodle over here. Enough of this delay, delay, delay. Capisci?

And just so you have a sense of the time-line of your task, yesterday was the deadline. So get moving Don Niccolo!"

"My men are…"

"Your men are what? Busy fighting amongst themselves? What kind of monkey-ass operation are you running over there? Years waisted. You are not only making your so-called Outfit look bad, but you are making me look bad in front of my superiors. And when they ruffle, dominoes fall, quickly my dear sir, very quickly. You think you have men on the job there in bumbfuk central? Let me assure you that when we send soldiers down range, their payment for a job well done is life spared. They are on the tarmac ready to jump at my word. So my dear friend, I don't give a canolli chocolate dip shit who is going to exercise this task, even if it is you. Or can you not get your polished finger nails grimy anymore? Time to go back to your slimy roots and giterdone!. Capisci!?"

"My grace, I…"

CLICK
"Chizzy! Get Enzo on the phone. NOW!!"

CHAPTER 16

ROOM AND BOREDOM

Atlanta, Illinois

A slow roll down dirt road 2350th Street kicked up less dirt. The 1976 champagne color Chrysler Imperial Le Baron crept along. The search more focused.

"Stop. Back a little. There, in the corn, that tractor path." Enzo pointed into the golden winter stalks.

Enzo and Nooli found the Lincoln Russell ditched. They got out and looked for trail sign in the dirt.

"Here, sneaker marks. Not work boots. Dumb shit never worked a day in his miserable life." Nooli examined the dirt signs close.

"Short life. Hehe. Looks like he got a gimp leg, Left tracks dragging." Enzo grunted. They followed the sign markings along the dirt road towards the I-55 overpass.

"He's in Atlanta." Enzo barely enunciated.

"Small enough. Nooli put the La Baron in gear."

"Let's go."

"Shall we get a room?"

"Probably. Can change clothes and blend in on foot."

"Down there, on the right. That spot there. Colaw Rooming House."

"Looks good."

The champagne Chrysler Imperial Le Baron found asphalt on NW Vine St.

The Colaw Rooming house, 204 NW Vine St in Atlanta. A beautiful early 19th century Victorian gingerbread two-story home converted into a rooming house. Coated in earth tone greens and browns, white trim, and large windows, it draws customers into its immaculate interior. Two brick fireplaces in the grand lobby warmed the soft tones leading to the grand oak staircase. The restored interior expertly detailed in an Early American style. Richly stained oak floors guide tenants directly into the American past. The unique in-laid patterns enhance the experience. The classic American furnishings compliment the ornamental floors. Lace drapes from ceiling to floor cover the wood-cased windows.

Enzo entered the house after shedding his shark skin Mickey Freeman suit jacket and tie. He put on a green and brown camo-mix overcoat, more appropriate for the location. Gloves added for effect.

"Howdy, needin a room?" An older man in winter plaid and jeans, wiry greyed out hair and deeply seasoned facial lines, greeted Enzo.

"Well I spose so. Me and my bud visiting a feed supplier for a few days of meetings and such." Enzo struggled to spit his best country boy accent.

"No problem. How long you need?"

"Not sure. These thangs can go quick or langer. Hoping supply truck be comin'in t'morra but ya know howz that kin be." Enzo struggled to keep up the accent over his mob-talian.

"I sure do bud. No worries. We a little slow there this week anyways."

"Great, don't be meanin'ta bother."

"No bother a'tall. Upstairs ok? We do have two on the first floor with a back door but a shared bathroom?"

"Even better. Don't wanna disturb anyone. You know how them rowdy farmers can be. Wanna throw a few back at the end of the day."

"Oh yea. No worries partner. What name you want to room under?

"It's corporate so you can use The Outfiters Inc. We outta Peoria."

"Oh yea I heard of y'all. You can pay cash or credit when you check out. Kitchen open if you cooking. Just be mindful of the others here. It's only Kevin here right now, he a regular. Always be scratchin with the wife Bella. He upstairs with his puppy, kellog. He keeps a bottle."

"Great. I'm Hank Mobley and may partner on this trip is Sam Cooke. Out in the car studying. He the smart one. Numbers guy."

"Gottcha. First door on the right. Here's the keys."

"Thanks. By the by, do you know a kid by the name of Russell Smerkers from 'round these parts?"

"Hmm. Can't say I do. Friend of yours?"

"Client, thanks."

Enzo headed back to the Chrysler, back on the search for clues, cutting more sign. Mindful not to draw too much attention, they eased the Imperial back onto Vine St. They turned on Arch St. as it looked to be the busiest. They cruised past the giant Paul Bunyon holding his giant hot dog. They considered going into Chubby's Bar and Grill, the prime bar tavern in town famous for cold beer and their signature pork tenderloin.

"Think he's in there?"

"He be visible as hell in there."

"Think he's that stupid?"

"Yup"

"Let's wait out here a minit, see if the idiot gets thrown out."

They curbed the Chrysler a block up by Top Flight Grain. Tucked in behind the grain silos next to the train tracks waiting on him to pop. A train sped by at 80 MPH.

"Fool be needing shelter if he on foot." Chick peered out of the passenger window of the Dragon easing down Arch street in Atlanta.

"Yea." Jimmy agreed from behind the wheel.

"Can you really trust that friggin Deacon?" Chick eyeballed every person he saw on the street.

"Of course not."

"Then why are we up here in Atlanta?"

"We got Atlanta and south back to town. Booker got in town with the legal team and Reese's crew said they got the rest."

"Man shit. Them African killers probably just want us out of the way so they can get all the glory for bringing his ass in."

"Booker has this thing mapped out like a grid. We go north. They stay south. It is their territory. They know all them nooks and crannies."

"Them African dudes is everywhere and nowhere. For all we know, they be up here in Atlanta now, dug in deep."

"Then what we doing here?" Chick lobbed a wad of spit out of the passenger window.

"Just chill man. You never know. That Greenwood church is up here too. Maybe we can recruit some of them to look out?"

"Oh yea! Deac said something about tips and tithes tables. They be getting it in up here. Sheeeiiit. Let's check'em out. May be a little trim up in there." Chick sat up straighter in the Dragon.

"Will you keep your strap on? You as bad as Deacon. Ain't no trim in this Atlanta cut. Gotta go to the Dirty Dirty for that. Ha! Magic City baby!"

"Awe c'mon man! I ain't strayed off this thing yet. How long we been here now?"

"Too long." Jimmy said as he looked at everything around him from behind the wheel.

"Too got damn long! That's wus I'm sayin. Like prison and shit."

"Keep your focus fool. Gotta get D out. This our only chance. Grab this fool, squeeze the truth outta him, then you can get back to your rotten tuna fish sandwiches."

"Fine."

"Where too? Ain't but so many other places to go up here."

What about that methodist church over there?"

"You know ain't no white boys in that church. If he's in there, he's an oddball fo sho."

"True. Let's keep on patrol. If he here in Atlanta, he'll pop up. You know he's paranoid."

- https://www.enjoyillinois.com/explore/listing/paul-bunyon-hotdog-statue/

Part 4

TACTICS

CHAPTER 17

HUMPTY DUMPTY

Atlanta

Deac. Where you at? Can't nobody get hold of yo'ass. You better not be up in no heifer's bladder," Booker scoffed inside of a phone booth, outside of Motel 7.

"Boy you have no idea. Them big one's is oooooooweee! And don't be judging me." Deacon dismissed Bookers's comments.

"Whatever. What's going on up there?"

"Well, for one, I ain't seen your boys yet. Probably got side tracked at the massage parlor. And two, I'm at my favorite spot, Missy's Sweet Shoppe across from the big dog man, near the church."

"I don't give a flying fuck where you at, what you got? Anything besides the clap?"

"Oh you got jokes this morning but I just got off of the Humpty Dumpty One-Ball and…

"Look, I don't have time for this, we lookin for the freakish white boy…

"That's what I'm tryna tell you if you would stop flappin your super-coolers and listen for once. Jezus, Jacob and Johnny Walker. Boy don't be listening! Don't know why I put up with you people. Anyways, this one-ball Humpty Dumpty pin ball machine is one of them real-deal old school machines that only uses one ball."

"DEAC!! I got one more nerve left!"

"Listen to me now! It's not for winning extra games, it's for winning extra cash bro, like a slot machine."

"Uh huh."

"Well, I like coming here to play it after being at the church. Cuz I usually have a few extra quarters after whippin up on them Jezus boys at the poker and craps tables in the church. I come here to get a horseshoe and a pop."

"I don't wanna know. Talkative ass mu'fukka. Dayum! Go on."

"Whatever. So this dude was on my machine so I had to wait and went and got a burger and ice cream soda, and you know how vanilla makes me lactose gasseeose?"

"DEAC GOTDAMNIT! GET TO IT MAN, SHIT!"

"Ok ok. Well I didn't pay much attention to the dude on MY machine until he started cussing at it. Then he banged on it and walked out all pissed off.

"So."

"Sooooo, it was that pimply faced shit head you lookin for. THAT'S WHAT IS SO!! BAM BITCHES! NOW WHAT! HUH? WHAT!?"

"Are you kiddin me right now? Don't be boolshittin me on this Deac!"

"Square biz Bozo. It's him as Moses is my witness."

"You sure?"

"Hellz to the yea. It was that same dip shit I saw at the Tiki lounge the night it burnt down. He was with them greasy dego-woppers."

"Did you follow him? Where is he?"

"Well ya see, the Humpty Dumpty came open when he left so I jumped on real quick..."

"YOU WHAT!?"

"But I hit on my first ball for twenty bucks! Paid for the burger and pop."

"I don't give a shit bout that! Where'd he go fool!"

"In my holy rapture excitement I didn't want to scream inside the quaint little shoppe so I went outside to let out my glorious joy and air out of my gaseosus from the vanilla shakepop. But I saw him go into the Hawes thing just down the street."

"The what?"

"The Hawes. The big red tall box elevator storage house thingy I told you about."

"Is he still in there?"

"I guess so. Ain't nowhere to go in this jacked town. If he on the run then he hunkered down in there.

"Look for the guys. Tell them about it but wait from me to get there. Meet up at the pop shop. I be there in fifteen minutes. Get a tail on him! Keep an eye on him till the fellas get there. I'm on my way now! Look for the fellas in the Dragon."

"Ok but I'm feeling lucky and I need to get back on the Humpty while my iron is hot."

"DEACON DAMIT!"

"It's ok. I gassed out all that vanilla pop outside when I was shouting out my glory victory to the Lord. The coast is clear." Deacon fanned the air in front of his nose inside the phone booth.

"Whatever."

"By the way. With this info I blessed you with, can you possibly see it to slide me a little something, say a hundred fifty? Ya see I promised my little Tiko a night out and i could use…"

"DEAC!"

"But she's an international hoe and…"

CLICK.

"Hello? Heathen."

- Atlanta Illinois, home of Missy's Sweet Shop and the Deacon's vices

  https://missyssweetshoppe.com/

CHAPTER 18

LIVE SHOT

WGN *Reporter Desiree Justine has the latest on the interracial adoption murder trial set to begin in Lincoln with this live report outside of the Logan County Courthouse in Lincoln. Desiree, I see there's lots of protesting going on there now even before the trial begins?"*

"Thanks Merri. Yes. As you can see behind me, there are protestors holding signs to free Darnell. As well, there are other signs saying things like, separate but equal and don't tread on me. But today marks the first day of jury selection in the capitol murder trial of Darnell Whitaker, who has been accused of killing his adopted mother and father. If you remember, Darnell Whitaker was the first African-American youth adopted by a white family in the state of Illinois, soon after the laws were changed, allowing for interracial adoption in the state. Seems this trial is full of small town drama with big city twists. The judge in the case, Howard McDougle will be presiding over the case that has Chicago lawyers in town prosecuting and defending. State Prosecutor, Robert Frongello, recently known for as a defense attorney for many members of the Chicago Outfit, to now becoming a prosecutor for the state. He will be facing off against the newly popular, up and coming trail blazing legal team for South Side justice, lead by attorney Percy Whitaker. To add even more drama, the defendant, Darnell Whitaker is attorney Whitaker's son!"

"Oh my! How did this happen? This is a twist."

"Indeed it is Merri. And to add more ingredients to the stew, Judge McDougle was attorney Whitaker's law professor at Northwestern."

"This just keeps getting better Desiree. Isn't there some conflict of interest here?"

"Oh that's not the half of it. Judge McDougle was the central arbitrator and facilitator of the interracial adoption of Darnell to the Wagner family here in Lincoln a few months back. He ensured the adoption went forward in the cloud of local, state, and federal debate about laws prohibiting interracial adoption."

"So wait? The judge brought the kid to Lincoln?"

"Yes. And if you want more twists Merri? The judge is the first cousin to the murder victim, Elizabeth Wagner and her husband Chuck. To top that off, Mrs Wagner was the great great great grand daughter of Abraham Lincoln."

"Oh my. There must be a conflict of interest there. Is the judge going to recuse himself?"

"Well, actually no. He has been cleared by the state judicial review board to proceed. Appears that sense he was acting in an official capacity in the adoption proceeding, the Illinois judicial review board voted unanimously to not recuse, citing no personal gain or bias involved. As well, McDougle's decades long reputation as a fair and impartial judiciary played a crucial role in their decision to not recommend recusal."

"Incredible."

"Yes Merri. This case is not without its unique sub-texts. The trial is setting up to be an explosive event."

"What's the word on the street?"

"Mixed reviews so far. Darnell is loved by so many here. Yet there are also many who believe he is guilty. Some are saying he is a joy and the spark this town needed. Many refuse to believe he did this horrible crime, killing his parents after just watching a movie together. Many didn't see a hurtful bone in his body. From school administrators to shop owners, farmers

and clergy, Darnell seems to have touched many of their hearts. Now those hearts are broken for the loss of the Wagners and the ugly future that could await Darnell if found guilty. With me now is Obediah Silver, a local Lincoln resident, born and raised right here in Lincoln, is that correct sir?"

"Uh hi. Uh yes ma'am. Born and bread right here in Lincoln. The hospital right over thar. My pappy born here and his pappy too and his mammy. I'm Lincoln through-n-through."

"Do you and your family and friends feel that the interracial law has worked here in light of this tragedy? Most people I spoke with say there were no issues with Darnell."

"One thang fer sher, you cain't mix no doggone goats wit pigs. Both are wonderful animals but God didn't make them the same. Ya, no wut'i'm'sayin? And we always been thanking this way here. Since the early days. This Darnello fella come in here looking round, doing thangs, askin bout thangs we do an'such. Yea we side-eyed him lots. But every time I go to the Wagners for anythang…parties, yard work, help out, events and the lak, that boy, well, he different ya no."

"You mean because he's black?"

"Naw. He see thangs differ-like. First he confuse the hell outta me…oh sorry we on the tee vee, oops…but I had trouble figurin him out. But I tell ya. Every time I come cross him, I start to see where he coming from ya'no? This dude the most charm'in smartness fella I knewed fo his age. He jus a kid. Ain't got no agenda on nuttin, ya'no? And he funny as all git out. He one hell of a basketball player too. Did you know that boy can play the hell out of a horn? That jazzy muzik. Yea! And when I seent him out and about by himself, he know how to talk to grown fokes, proper lak. And he always reading them funny books. He showd me this one called Black Panther. Shoot. I got bout twenty them thangs now. Git'em from mayer Dez at his shop jus over thar cross the yard there. Cain't put'em down."

"So you think interracial adoption is a good thing?"

"I ain'ts no lawyerin or social scientific type but all I be knowd is people ain'ts horses, goats nar pigs. Well, some are sheep and I do know this one gal that could pass for a prize hog... he he he! Jus kiddin thar. I tickled myself somethin. But naw, I mean yea. With Darnello, it's a darn good thang. Animals go in the barn. People go in yer head. That's why I'm down here today. That boy ain't killdt nobody. I don't thank he ever tolda a fib in his entire laf. I don't thank he knowd how'ta lie. He likes to free mice when they in the barn traps. I mean hell, who does that? They need to stop all this nonsense and free that boy. He can come live with me. Shoot, he probably run the farm for me. I work for him. Lots of stuff I don't know bout and a real man ain't shame to admit what he don't know. A fool thank he know it when he don't. Don't matter what ya look lak. It's what ya saying and how ya be treatin fokes an wut yuh showing what yuh be doin. Know what i'm saying? Shoot."

"Well thank you Mr. Silver."

"Jus call me Obie. Dat short for Obadiah."

"Thank you Obie. And there you have it. Lots to unpack there. And so much more to come from this. Reporting live from the Lincoln Courthouse grounds during the start of the Darnell Whitaker murder trial for WGN, I'm Desiree Justine. Back to you Merri."

"Wow! Thanks Obie, I mean Steve. That was incredible.

"No problem Ms. Justine. My pleasure working with you again. My train back to Chicago is at 4:50. Should put me back downtown in time to make my curtain call at the Goodman Theater by 8. It was indeed an honor, truly. I need to get this latex off my face. Starting to itch."

"Sorry we went long. You were on a roll. I almost lost it. Your check has been deposited. Masterful sir."

"All good. I keep getting me these type gigs, lov'em. Guess I'm type casted now. I wanted to do more romantic roles, be a Sidney Poitier type, but ya do wut ya gotta do to get by in this craft. Can't be too picky. And this is so much fun Desiree. Thank you again for the opportunity."

"Your name is synonymous with professionalism. Not bad for an Italian boy from South Philly. Take care Steve. You are like Steve Austin, the six million dollar man. I don't know how you do it sir."

"Ayyyee, that jawn was the goods. Later chick."

"Well? What ya think? Shot look good?" Desiree confirmed with her videographer, Donovan.

"Yea. Nice. I need to get more b-roll of the positive signs and faces. Gotta keep the Klansmen out of my shots. They're so disgusting. You need to check in with Percy. He'll be calling in from the secure roof phone in five minutes on that pay phone over there. I'll be shooting more of this mess out here."

Donovan shut off his camera light. Packed up the live TV gear. Stripped down his camera equipment to ENG style for run and gun video shooting. He says that's where the art is. Not this bullshit on sticks with lights.

Percy, JC and Abe were nose deep in documents studying the gaggle of potential jury members. 18 men. 18 women. No African-Americans in the pool. They needed to pick their nine. Will let Frongello select his corrupt nine first. Certain he will choose all men on the take. The team focused on the women.

Percy went to the roof.

RIIINNNGGG

"Did you see it?" Desiree asked Percy from the pay phone on the corner of Broadway and McLean.

"Hold on Dray, going put connet you to the office phone from this roof phone so they can hear. Standby to be on speaker." Percy made his way back down from the City Hall roof phone booth.

"Gerl, that dude was masterful, incredible! You were so right about him. This is why you may just get that slow dance when we get back," Percy glowed at the speaker-phone on the conference table after the successful media hit tactic.

"Oh Percy you are such a tease. You want that dance with or without underwear?" The three defenders laughed at Desiree's nasty mouth.

"Will they be clean?" The room howled.

"Clean enough daddy, sheeeiiit. What you want? A bag of cotton balls or a box of nasty alley cats! HA!!!" The room roared again.

"Pigs and goats?!? Really? I ain't no lawyerin or social scientific type but all I know is people ain't sheep, goats or pigs? This dude needs to be in Hollywood and not in the local theaters back home. Freeing mice in the barn? Who thinks of this stuff?" Said Percy.

"I told you he's my go to didn't I? To think he grew up in Philly talking like Rocky? And his dark olive skin and thick black hair never came through the make-up. No one will ever know who that dude is. I'm just glad Barbara called me after Butch let her know about McDougle and the board's decision." Said Desiree.

"And his role in the adoption." JC added.

"Gave me good meat for the bone gerl. Sheeeiitt Percy, when you gonna unleash all that other incriminating shit I gave you from the hotel? I want to start my expose with the Tribune on that ass-hole."

"Amazing stuff Desiree. All of that stuff on him is an aside that should go national, but not yet. First things first. How often will this one air?" Abe leaned in closer to the speaker phone.

"Four or five times today. They may use bites in the teases throughout the day. But we gotta keep feeding the beast or it dies of cardiac complacency and distraction inside the news cycle. Gotta stay on top of the cycle." Desiree fidgeted in the phone booth, looking around for any repercussions from the antsy-crowd gathering around the court house.

"Now we move on to phase three. This is the last call on this line. They will be pissed in a few minutes after that performance. Expect line tapping to commence any time now. From now on it's on the clock and on the roof only. Got it?" Percy gave more stern orders to the team.

"We on it. See you on the little screen! Smooches my nigga!" Desiree exited the phonebooth power walking across the courthouse grounds amongst the protestors looking for more sound.

"Why does she keep calling us her nigger?" Yuri adjusted his slipping yarmulke.

"It's a term of endearment when used that way. You'll catch on Yuri. Let's get back to it. We have two more hours before we go in for jury select. Frongello is in there now. Probably handing out Benjamins like Halloween candy. Let's get this done. We already know the outcome. Just need to know these women's histories so we can squeeze it." Said Percy.

The team got back to work.

- Battleground set

CHAPTER 19

SIDE 2 SIDES

Defense HQ, City Hall

The D-Team reassembled in their office in City Hall South after jury selection. Barbara and Desiree met the team inside coming through a counsel chambers back entrance through the fire department back door.

"Well that went as expected. Plenty of theater from Frongello's team. And they acted as expected. All men selected. All cashed out I'm sure. See how adamant they were and even coached to say the tactfully ambiguous yet passively aggressive stance about his guilt. So Mob-like predictable." Percy filled his coffee cup, extra sugar pour.

"Right. They were quite cocky. I hope we got the women we want. Tough call down here." JC joined him at the coffee counter.

"Abe, do you think Mrs. Dewhau was transparent?

"Considering her father and uncles are Klan members and her grand father was killed in Chicago race riots, I suppose. She has enough in her to call him guilty with the right pressure. But she stood on her high school career teaching U.S. history and civics giving her more objectivity to truth. I guess we will see."

Barbara grabbed an everything bagel, calculating something in her head.

"Desiree, what's your feel for the crowd outside now?"

"Tough crowd. I get the historical DNA around here. Mixed emotions in them. But without a significant population of minorities here, most will always lean to the right. Like they are the victims, protecting something. It comes up more often than not. I totally feel a broader conspiracy for those on the guilty side. It's in your face and out the mouth ridiculous with so many of them."

"How so?"

"They all seem to have similar talking points. They say things like; you never know about those poor city folk, code words for blacks guilty; some people never had love in their lives, code for blacks guilty; foster children have convicts for fathers and drug addicts for mothers, code for blacks guilty; some people don't know how to act when they are confronted with something different, like a fish out of water, can't swim, code for black guilty. Same same same same from that side all day. Everywhere I went out there. Like a broken record. And they appeared to be so unified with their posters and placement around the court house grounds. Like it is highly organized and not a loose gathering like the other side. Pods of sheep on each corner surrounding others, covering the walkways so they can blast the messages in your ears when you walk by them."

"Where is all this coming from?" JC asked.

Barbara spoke up. "I tell ya what. The Black community is all on board with Darnell, of course. I've been to the churches all around here. To the colleges, factories, farms, stores, talking to black people about it. Feeling them out. And they all fear he will be convicted even though he is innocent. They've been telling me about meetings of whites-only at the work places after work, seeing them come out of the meetings acting different."

"I mean damn! The not-guilty protestors outside feel like the normal people of town. They are all about freedom for

Darnell. They say Darnell wouldn't hurt a fly. They all seem to know him. And the other side, they don't seem to know him at all, just of him. They are the worse elements of town. You saw them out there, bunch of renegades, moronic thugs. Cursing and shit like they are in a bar or at a rodeo," Desiree paced the floor while talking.

"But you know who you did not see out there?" Barbara asked.

"Who?" Yuri plated two bagels with lox and extra creme cheese.

Barbara paused, careful with what she was about to infer.

"Leadership. Where are all of our town leaders?"

"Like who?" Percy sat at the study table one eyebrow up, in serious wonder, awaiting the answer.

"Well how about the Mayor for starts? Where is Bartmiester? All these crazy events that have happened here over the last month. Some of the biggest things that have happened around here since Lincoln went off to DC. Everybody came out for that messy event, top to bottom. But now I don't see anyone accept the bottom. Where the hell is Ron Keller, Paul Beaver, LaDaris Knauri, Bernardo Barons, William Martinie, Raymond Keys, Floyd Durst, and Joe Funk? These are the town leaders. They have businesses that can be adversely affected by a negative outcome. I don't get it." Said Barbara

"But will they?"

"Will they what Percy?" Barbara asked.

"Be adversely affected by a guilty verdict. Or will they prosper?"

"That just don't make no damn sense." JC rose from the table.

"Wait. What if it makes perfect sense?" Yuri talked through the lox and bagel dough in his mouth.

"The hell you talking about Yuri?"

"Think about it. If what you say makes perfect sense, that they stand to loose if Darnell goes down, then of course that is financial suicide. Horrible negative press on a small town in the middle of nowhere needing tourism when the farm revenues are all over the place. No growth. No taxes, etc. But thinking conversely, what would they stand to gain if he goes down?"

Silence in the room.

"Think about it. If the major players are all involved in some crazy plot that gains them some pot of gold in the end, then they want this to play out."

"But how and what does Darnell have to do with anything so broad and massive?" JC asked.

"Don't know. That has always been the X factor in every road block we run into. Now it appears to be a common denominator, right? Somebody somewhere is spinning up some golden soup laced with the poison of death. The elixir is so devilishly relish that they would sacrifice a lamb to get it. The payoffs need to be huge. On a giant scale." Yuri pushed.

"Like from here to Bloomington? To Clinton? Mason City? Williamsville?

I guess I have my targets now." Desiree sucked her teeth like a salivating hyena. She peered over at Donovan. He moved with the serious smoothness of a puma on the hunt, grabbing his camera gear. Checking his battery power, tacking up like an Army ranger. Strapping up to hit the streets to hunt for zombies. They all looked at each other.

"Holy shit!" JC started digging through her papers.

"These muther Fukkers! I can't believe it." Yuri scrambled breaking open one of his three overstuffed clunky leather briefcases.

Percy stood from the table.

"Just a minute! Hold yourselves. Before we go down this road, we either link Darnell to this or we save it for a rainy day. I'm not saying we don't dig for a broad conspiratorial connection, but let's not over burden ourselves with filing conspiracy charges yet. Let's get him free first. Then be ready to slap charges later. We may need to go back home to develop all of this." Said Percy.

"Shit, then we will be living down here like Darnell if we bring this?" JC sulked.

"What I have on tape from McDougle in the hotel is straight blood juice." Desiree paced back and forth.

"Let's slow our roll a bit here. If we go there, then it's for the long haul. We will need more than this little posse here and the fellas in the streets." Percy held up his hands like stopping traffic.

"We have the Deacon!" Yuri brought levity to the team. They all hollered in relief of pent up stress and emotion.

"And yes we have the Deacon, God help us all. So let's keep our eyes on this prize. Cuz in reality folks, we are up against it knowing what we know now. This deck is stacked high. We going against the mob with a racist referee who hates all of us, remember? We need to be ready to focus on the appeal. Maybe that gives us time to build out the mass conspiracy theory. I mean, ask yourselves how big could it really be down here? Then multiply that times the Outfit. We will need a miracle to save my boy. We gotta dig deeper people."

Quiet rested the room. The air-condition kicked on and it's the middle of December. The team got busy building their case and readying for opening arguments.

Desiree and Donovan geared up in the corner of the room, developing their new attack for round-three of news gathering, Chicago style.

- HQ Defense Team S.S. - Lincoln City Hall. Site of the rooftop phone booth

- Yup, it's still there!

CHAPTER 20

ATLANTA SEARCH

Atlanta, Illinois
Missy's Sweet Shop

"Deac! Where you at?" Jimmy stormed into Missy's Sweet Shoppe.

The vintage 1950's stylized soda shop with the black and white checkered tile floors, chrome padded bar stools, and stocked display cases of rows and rows of cookies, cakes and sweets, and the one-ball machine, the Deacon's camp out now.

"Keep your voice down. This is a fine establishment, and I need to concentrate on my pinball."

"Where is he?" Chick pushed Deacon.

"Ya'll hungry? They got great Horseshoes and Cherry Coke pop here."

"I don't want no damn horse meat. I want white boy meat. Now where is he!" Jimmy jammed him in the shoulder.

"Shhhh, you scare'in the locals. By the way, did you bring that one-fifty? My little Tiko is particular about her seaweed."

"I'm warning you! Don't make break my foot off in your ass!" Chick pulled Jimmy back.

"So hysterical. Chill out bubble butt."

"Chick, check this fool before I wreck his ass."

"Look here Deac, stop play'in. Where'd he go?" Chick tried to settle things down in front of the local patrons sipping ice-cream floats and chomping down on Missy's famous pumpkin bars, trying not to stare at the odd acting black men.

"Ok ok. Follow me outside. I'll show you where I saw him hobble off to."

"Hobble?" Jimmy asked.

"Well he couldn't seem to walk to good. Either a limp or a pimp and that pimply face bastard fosho ain't no P-I-M-P. If so, then I'm boutta run this whole mutha from the Link to the drink baby!."

"Shut up! Just show us where. Got damn! Can't you keep your dick off the corner for five minutes?"

"Jus'shut up and follow me, team doofs. But those snicker doodles do smell good. I made need a dozen. Tiko has a sweet tooth. Where's your glorious leader, Bookman Marcelious?"

"He's in the phone booth. Let's go!"

"What, changing into his blue tights and cape?"

Deac lead the crew one block down SW Arch St. to Race st., then a quick left on SW First. Booker followed.

"This the Red Wing Bowling Alley, they sell that corn liquor and them Indian cigs. I'll be working on my hook in here then bust yall's asses some more."

"DEAC!"

"And here it is. The J.H. Hawes Elevator. A grain elevator now a friggin museum, talk about bumfuck? Museums suppose to have wax figures and vending machines. This is just weird."

"Shut up." Chick blasted and went into creep mode. He eased up to a side door of the tall red wooden structure.

"Jimmy, go around to the back. I got the other side." Booker gave quiet commands.

Deac started to back away. Not wanting to get involved.

"That's the Greenwood church hangout over there." Deac pointed across the street to the red brick Methodist church building. "I'll be heading back there to pick up Tiko. Then we going to the Route 66 Arcade Museum just down the block. Gonna teach her the fine art of the game. I'll be in there if you be needin me and my greatness."

"Stay your ass right here." Booker signaled him to keep quiet.

At 3pm, the 1907 six-story four-sided stone clock tower next to the town library rang out three pounding clangs. The team startled.

Crows perched on the second floor of the J.W. Hawes scattered. The clanging forced them to fly crazily out of the top of the building's windows.

Jimmy pushed open a creaky side door under the noise of the birds and bells' disruption. Chick slipped in through another doorway as Jimmy eased through the front side of the grain harvesting area. Booker went around back.

Sun rays filtered through the old structure. Its rays poked through holes in the rotting wooden red walls and roof. The crows spun up dust ferries that twinkled in the sun ray's glow above them. The team peered around the aged grain equipment for Russell. Chains from the upper level that once hoisted the grain elevator platform up to a second-story conveyor slide, clanked in the stirred up moldy air inside.

The guys converged inside the creaky building quietly, looked at each other with negative success in their eyes.

A noise grabbed their attention on the second floor. Chick lead the climb to the top with Jimmy. Book went back outside behind an old train car adjacent to the building incase Russell tried to jump from the top onto it.

Chik poked his head out of a top floor opening where the grain once poured out and filled the train car below. He shook his head, nothing. Jimmy looked around for clues in the upper deck. Nothing.

"Yo. Check this out" Chick dug through some items in a small equipment closet.

"His stuff. Look at this. I think our little bird has a broken wing," Jimmy showed them a rag with dried blood.

"Yea and he flew the coop. But he's on foot. Here's some car keys, can't go too far without these." Booker pocketed the keys.

"He gone." Chick said.

"He may be watching us." Jimmy looked up and down inside the Hawes.

"He's busted up." Booker confirmed sifting through his rags and items in the closet. "But he's not sleeping here. No stuff like that here. This was a stop-over under cover. He must have ditched the car to be up here in Atlanta."

"But why was he here?" Jimmy asked.

"Hmm. Deac said he was pissed off cuz he didn't win on pinball. Why was he playing pinball with a busted leg? Especially after what he did?"

"He broke." Deacon slipped in.

"What?"

"He broke. Needs money. Those old style pinballs pay cash if you win. Maybe 20 bucks. I tied to tell ya'll stank asses." Deac giggled walking away.

"And he lost. So he ain't far. Let's go. He's here some where. I can feel it. We going eyeballing." Booker commanded.

- Atlanta, Illinois Hawes Grain Elevator Museum
- https://destinationlogancountyil.com/grain-elevator-museum

CHAPTER 21

BED ROLL

7:00am, Lincoln Lock Up

"When I'm sleeping at night
I have visions of you
I make believe we runnin away
To a world of fantasy
Pretty images of you
Are reflected on the clouds in the sky
You appear as an angel from heaven
Bringing love and ecstasy"

Hi officer Bruce. Is Darnell up?" Maria startled Officer Butler who was napping to his music in his chair at the jail.

"Uh, uh, oh hey Maria. Sorry. Must have dozed off. What?"

"Cool song. Who's that?"

"Oh that's the Blackbyrds. A D.C. group. What's up?"

"Smooooth. Like your bald head. Is he up? I know it's a little early but I want to get an early start."

"I think so. Hey D-man. You up?" Maria called out as she made her way to Darnell's open cell.

Darnell rolled over in his bunk, rubbing his eyes. "I am now."

"Yup he's up." Bruce reacted down the hall.

"Thanks baldo."

"Watch it Missy." Bruce went back to dozing.

Maria plopped a bag of comics down on the bunk.

"Hey! What time is it?" Darnell stretched his jail-bunk achy body.

"Wakey wakey eggs and bakey. Time to rise and shine in the big time."

"You call this big time?"

"Well this is making you a celebrity ya'no. Everybody talking about Darnell Darnell Darnell."

"Darnell who?"

"Well you may not know him but I know this bad ass mofo from CheeCaGo."

"Must you this early? Do you ever rest?"

"Rest shmest. I'll rest when you're outta here. I brought you a new set of the latest Sub Mariner, Lightening, Surfer, Dr. Strange, and stuff. Dez's supply is kinda lightfoot now days. He needs to order newer stuff. I peeped his inventory records and he hasn't ordered anything in months. I'll check him on that later. In the mean time, I found this old thing called Lion Boy. Thought of you."

Darnell snatched the book from her. "Let me see that!"

"Oh. Wait. I'll be back. Need to get some things off my bike. Darnell dug into the 1942 #41 edition of Lion Boy with great curiosity. Maria came back with a paper bag.

"And what is that?" Officer Butler peered over his news paper and coffee mug at Maria re-entering the station.

"Oh. My mom made you a special fat-rito breakfast burrito, double stuffed with fluffy cheesy huevos, sausage, bacon, onions, and she put that Tajin seasoning in it, just for you, officer fat-ass. She says you deserve the best breakfast so you can do your best for ole meat-head in there."

"What's tagreen?"

"That's Tajin? It's a Mexican seasoning with chili, lime, pepper and stuff. I don't know but it's the bomb-diggity yo!"

"Hmm."

"Here ya go fat boy."

"Hey. I resemble that remark," he smiled peeling open the foil-wrapped fat-rito, tearing into it.

"Well? Well? Good right?" She stared a him for approval of the food.

"Oh damn! Is your mom actually divorced? Cuz I be like over yall's house tonight if she can hook a brother up like this on a regular. Does she like robust baldheaded black cops with beards? I can shave it off."

"You so stupid. And I don't know but you cannot be my father. You too old and smelly, That would mean I would have a maroon brother or sister."

"Exactly what medications are you on? Loony pills? Maroon siblings? What are you talking about?

"Hey, what color does black and brown make? Maroon?"

"Shut up and get outta my face. I got Tajin to devour."

"Fat boy! Ha! My mom will run circles around your bald nugget." She scurried down the hall back to the cell.

"Like it? Or lame-O?" She put down the bag of breakfast foods and a bed roll.

"Do you know what this is?"

"What?"

"This Lion Boy?"

"Nope. Who is Lion Boy again? Didn't you mention this before? I grabbed it cuz I thought of you."

"Oh My God. Does Dez know you have this?"

"I guess. I just dumped a bunch of books on the counter and he rang it all up quickly. He had to get his smoked butt again. Ya no Dez and his smoked butt."

"Ha!! Yea. I gotta pee. Anyway, Lion Boy was a baby when he was in an airplane crash in the African jungle. He was found by a lioness and she raised him with the pack. Later when he was older, he found the plane wreck. He didn't remember any of it but he made a knife from the some of the metal of the wreckage. He later killed the pack's alpha male in a fight. He then became ruler of the pack. This book is the last one produced. Dez would poop himself if he knew he sold you his only copy."

"Well, let the toilet paper fly baby cuz there's a new Lion King in the house! Here, this is for you."

"What's this?" Digging into the brown paper bag she handed him.

"Chow-burgers."

"What's all that other stuff?"

"This is my camping gear. Shoot. Wait I forgot something." She dropped her bed roll and ran back down the hall and outside. Bruce didn't look up from his next bite. Cheesy eggs in his beard.

"You got any hot sauce?" He called to her as she raced by him again.

Maria ignored him running out the door. She came back with a long metal object in her hand. She dropped a bottle of Don Peppe's Habanero sauce on Bruce's desk without stopping.

"What's that bike tire pump for?" Darnell asked.

"My air mattress." She unrolled the deflated air mattress, sheet, Mexican blanket, and small pillow on the floor.

"Ummmm. Can you???."

"Gotta have the creature comforts. For the long haul. You hold it down on the inside, I got the outside. Then we strategize at night. Dig?"

"Can you do that?"

"I'm doing it. So here's how I see it. I ain't no lawyer or cop, so my part is to keep you fed and informed. I can listen to the ground and get you the grub hub."

"Grub hub? Can you stop making up words?"

"Shut up. I'm talking, anyway. I'll get the snacks and stuff and see what these rednecks are blabbing about. Get a polaroid."

"Get what? Never mind. Dang. What's in these potatoes?"

Voices down the hall and steps headed their way stoped the chatter.

"What the hell is all this!? A kiddy tea party? What you think you doing young lady? We ain't running no damn daycare here," Sheriff Tucker stood in the cell doorway.

"Officer Butler thought it would be a good idea if we can hang out during all of this. Keep his spirits up, ya no?"

"He did, did he? Bruce!? You ok this campfire?"

Butler came down the hall.

"Um, well she brings breakfast and…"

"Yes sir. You are absoluto correcto. This is not a daycare center. But I do bring the minor age perp breakfast and water since the water cooler is empty. And the officer must stand his post. I get the minor-aged perpetrator food in this adult prison. And I bring this child reading materials. Since there are none of those. All of these are requirements for this class of youth detainee. Reading the City Jail statues at work, Counsel-Woman Sizemore asked if I could assist you with these to stay in compliance with the City and State statutes. Since Darnell and I are friends, I understand his needs better than you busy important adults and stuff." Twirling her hair.

"Umm hmm."

"Just keeping his spirits up sir. These lock-downs are temporary with few liberties and I totally get that, but there are certain civil requirements we must maintain for youth detainees, according to the statutes. I know you are very busy protecting us. I want to take some of the burden off you and your department by providing this youth with essential services, since Lincoln does not have any facilities for youth protection during this class of detention period. With all do respect sir, with all of these high powered lawyers and media buzzing around, I didn't want any attention to come down on your department, our department, and our city, for child abuse or anything like that. I can keep the vultures away while you guys keep the criminals and lawyers off of us citizen soldiers. I read about something called the ACLU? They can be a nasty bunch of sharks looking to feed off of a small town police department like ours. Even that NAACP bunch is down here snooping around looking out for any violation of Black civil rights. I mean after what this country has been through with assignations and law suits, and rioting and stuff. Man, we need to keep this thing nice and cozy-like and off the friggin radar. If they get a hold of this crap in here, it will stink like an unfleshed tern. My little job at counsel is hard enough. I can't imagine what you are going through right now sir. Just doing my job sir. Just doing my job. Know what I mean Sheriff?"

Sheriff Tucker looked at her, Darnell, Bruce, the floor, to the upper left, scratched his balding head.

"Ok. But don't let this get out. I mean what would the other lock-ups think if they saw this set up?"

"Sir, we don't have any other lock-ups. Haven't in 10 months. And that was the Jake the drunk, for fighting himself outside of the station," Butler wiped eggs from his beard to hide his grin.

"With all this going on outside now, we just might." Tucker stood up straighter. Greasing up my Sir Gallagher Knight Stick just in case. Can never be too prepared ya'no? Aint gonna be no riots on my watch. Hell naw!" Tucker pulled up his gun belt.

"No sir! Not on your watch! We don't want Darnell saying bad things about us," Maria looked at all three, hands on her hips, glaring with authority at Darnell.

"Ok. Just don't let this get out of control. Bruce, keep and eye on this little pow wow. Let me know if the AUCLAAPC comes sniffing around. And for God's sake don't let them back here. Especially that snooping media monkey chick running around shoving microphones in peoples faces. I'd like to shove it up her fat ass."

Maria snickered.

"Yessir. Will do."

Tucker went back to his office grabbing things then back out to his car in a hurry. They stood frozen as he came and went. Bruce looked at Maria, rolled his eyes and walked away shaking his head.

"Who are you?" Darnell looked at her baffled.

"Student of the game baby. Student of the game. Hollywood if Holly could. Don't forget where I'm from. Dig me? You don't grow old being no fool."

"Old? Is all that stuff true?"

"Hey everybody got rights ya no. Sounded good though, right? I mean doesn't my asshole have rights?"

"What drugs are you on?"

"So let's talk strategy." She Indian squatted on her bed roll.

"Uggghh."

Bruce settled back in his chair. He sprinkled more Don Peppe's on his fat-rito. Put his black Chino boots up on his desk. Chomped down on his second fat-rito savoring the Tajin, with a snicker and quiet chuckle he turned up the radio.

- Negotiating and influencing, a Lincoln art

CHAPTER 22

THE TRIAL

December 22 - First day of winter

The line at the courthouse wrapped around the building. Sheriff Tucker, officers Sullivan and Butler did their best to keep the crowd calm. With no more room inside, some were yelling to bring the trial outside. One protestor walked around with a noose on a pole.

The buzz and chatter inside was more a roar now as the proceeding was already forty-five minutes delayed from starting. McDougle appeared worried this would get out of hand. His constant hammering of the gavel became useless. The pounding was no longer being heard through the anxious crowd buzz in the courtroom gallery that sounded more like the ocean pounding the shore. The Illinois granite walls reverberated the sound like a hovering helicopter.

The extended delay happened soon after the bailiff announced the judge. Attorney Frongello had to run and retrieve a missing folder. McDougle allowed it, unheard of as the pro-Darnell camp in the gallery became increasingly upset. Shouting and finger pointing across the isle was becoming more threatening. McDougle's anger promised to clear the courtroom but it never happened. This was an intentional move to throw early chaos into the mix. He wanted the jury to see how scary and intimidating the anti-Darnell faction can be. He hoped the antics would stoke enough fear in the jury to avoid a hung jury or not-guilty verdict and elevate their fears for their safety. Darnell nervously sat at the defense table twisting and turning. He fearfully looked for anyone who may want to come at him.

Frongello rushed back to court apologizing amongst the shouting and cursing. He asked for forgiveness from McDougle. Percy immediately objected and asked for an immediate suspension of the trial to another day or to have the gallery immediately thrown out. McDougle overruled his objection. The gallery settled down. Percy, JC and Yuri were furious. Percy winked at Darnell and his team with confidence, encouraging them to relax.

The bailiff and McDougle intimidated the crowd to simmer down so opening remarks can begin. Frongello constructed a pattern of violence in Darnell's past on the Chicago South Side from a very young age. He claimed he was bread for violence. He went into Darnell's day-one arrival behavior in Lincoln witnessed by many. He dug into Darnell's dissatisfaction of being adopted by a white family. Citing incarceration statistics of black juveniles growing up without fathers. How more important it was for Councilman Whitaker to pursue his personal goals than to raise his own son in a violent area of the city. That he would rather turn his son over to the authorities. Percy objected to this but McDougle overruled saying it wiil be allowed during opening arguments but warned Frongello to not bring in personal attacks against the defense council during the witness questioning phases.

Frongello continued citing witness after witness who will testify to Darnell's threats of violence towards white people before and after watching the movie at the Lincoln Theater. How he was egged on by the movie portraying negative black stereotypes. How Hollywood has put black people in a negative light throughout its history citing movie after movie, from Uncle Tom's Cabin to Gone with the Wind, and now this movie Soul Man. How Darnell was raised with negative and violent reactionary images in his head from TV, movies and real life in his neighborhood laden with drugs, gangs, prostitution, and fighting. He goes on discussing the day of the murders. How many people heard him at several locations talking loudly about threatening to blow up the town. How he will shoot the racists in the head with silver bullets. Indicating that he has a gun on him. Insisting that his violent DNA came to the surface as he began to see some elements in town that he perceived as racially dangerous. How his only resort was to react the way he was trained. Then he watched the movie, Soul Man, which some agree is a blatant stab in the eye of the black community. Allowing a white student to steal the only Harvard Univerity pre-law school scholarship for black high scool seniors in Los Angeles. This was the watershed event that set him off.

He pivoted to how the Wagners' did everything they could to exorcize his violent past out of him. Giving, showing, teaching, loving him in a way he has never seen or felt. A testament to their angelic make up and intent. He admitted that they were over their heads believing they could change him saying, *"Oh how wrong they were. Overwhelming proof that the passage of the interracial adoption law should not have happened. That America is not ready for these type of families."* Listing the black civic organizations that were adamantly opposed to the law's passage and how he worked to get it stopped because he understood that it cannot work, but only harm black children. He told of Councilman Whitaker's affiliation with these groups like the NAACP, the Urban League, ACLU, Urban League, the Black Panthers, Black Teachers Union of Chicago and the violent Black Muslims of Chicago. Percy's team never looked up from their copious note taking.

After 45-minutes of this non-sense, Frongello yielded the floor. Percy rose slowly, walking towards the jury saying nothing. Scanning their eyes. Connecting with the men on the take like he knew what they did. They diverted their eyes. He walked toward the gallery of pro-Darnell attendees and shook his head in disgust, clinched his mouth in frustration with them.

"You see what we are up against?" He approached the jury. McDougle warned him against theatrics and to stick to the law. Percy turned to his supporters rolled his eyes. They snickered. McDougle hammered the gavel for order.

"Ladies and *any* gentlemen of the jury," the crowd snickered again. Gavel hammered.

"Order!"

"Welcome to the show. Not a circus, but a show and tell display of two alternate universes. One, in a galaxy far far way. So far away that we mere earthlings are not able to see it or even travel there yet. Maybe one day Luke and Princess Leia will fly in and pick us up. Or maybe when a tracker beam locks on our coordinates, breaking down our molecules to digital particles transferring us to the magical mystical place where the prosecution holds dominion over its lowly ignorant earthly slaves." Gavel hammering.

"Mr. Whitaker, please."

"In the other universe, there's the Milky Way Galaxy, a solar system of nine planets, or so. And inside the asteroid belt, parked in the sweet spot of a fully sustainable biological carbon based world. A place where all creatures are touched by a living loving and forgiving God. Where his ultimate creations live in his image."

"Mr. Whitaker, must we?"

"Of course your honor. What you must ask yourself is, where do you live? Here or there? Here we live in reality. This reality we are confronted with today is a simple one. A reality with today's question at its core. Can a young man of intelligence, kindness, humor, various skills, a gift of gab, and leadership qualities, who shares a fully transparent life and love with many of you, be capable of destroying everything he has over a fiction movie? A very young person who has zero history of mental illness. Zero history of violence. Zero history of perpetual lying. Zero history of showing blatant disrespect towards his elders, teachers, shop owners, farmers, strangers or parents? So let's examine the facts of this case and side-bar the common sense and humanity part for a moment.

Fact. Darnell did not have a gun that day. Fact. He has never even fired a gun. Fact. The Wagner's only had two hunting rifles in the house, no hand guns. Fact. Darnell is a comic book aficionado. Fact. He is a master at the craft of reading and comprehending the many plots, sub plots, characters, and fantastic stories within the universe of comics. He became a proven community partner and obvious future leader, fact! And yes he is my son. All facts. Some of you may say this comic book stuff is not reading. So I ask you, what are words and pictures on a page but a story, a tale, a report of some kind? And what do humans in this universe do with these elements? They read them. Process them. Interpret them. Darnell has been reading, processing and interpreting the written word since he was two years old, as I taught him to read at that age. Thus he has a highly expanded capability to read and comprehend words, and distinguish fact from fiction. Darnell has never travelled to any of those comic universes, physically or mentally. Not by intergalactic ship. Tracker beam. Mind transfer. None. Facts. I would have known. He would have at least brought back moon rocks."

More hammering. "Get on with it Mr. Whitaker! For the love of God."

"Yet somehow, those in the alternate universe here are certain that a young boy with this history actually did the most heinous crime known to man? All of us in this court room know better." He peered at McDougle. A red eyed, red headed glare returned his stare.

"Yes I am here to free my son. Yes this is an extremely difficult and personal task. Did I consider having someone else represent him? Yes, but my better angles said otherwise. I am here to fight for my son like I have never fought for him before. I don't need to apologize or explain myself to any of you. God and my team know what I have been doing in my son's life for the past five years. The prosecution would have you believe I abandoned my son for my own self interest. It is true that I completed my law degree and started my own practice since leaving my son and his mother. And I thank the Honorable Judge McDougle for teaching me the technical aspects of practicing the law. Matter of fact, his excellent teachings completely influenced me to not return home. He always said there is nothing more important than the law. And if you want to be a lawyer, a good lawyer, you may have to give up many things you love and replace them with your love of the law, if you want to be successful. You told us that your Honor. Remember?"

McDougle did not respond.

"You must put it all out there. Is what he use to tell us young law students. As a matter of more fact, my entire team you see here today are students of Judge McDougle. So we are all one big happy family here today." Snickers and giggles from the entire gallery.

Hammering.

"This family affair is like many families. Some bickering, disfunction, differences, testing limits. We all have been there with our loved ones. And we all have been pushed into various corners by them. Sometimes we act like cornered ally cats, lashing out, clawing, raging for survival. Anything to get out of that corner. But I venture to say that most of us who truly love our families may puff up and make noise and show our teeth and maybe scratch our loved ones from time to time. Some may choose to separate from them physically. Run away so no more hurt happens to them. But I venture to say every person in here today, practically no matter the circumstances, would still maintain a love connection with those family members you scratched. No matter how testy they become towards you. No matter how far away you may be from them. No matter how you may have hurt them. God put in us the ability to stay in love with each other no matter the circumstances.

So I rise before you today to show you and my son that I am not the disconnected self-serving father the prosecution would have you believe that I am. To prove to you that Darnell is not the violent angry young black boy who only knows hate, distrust, lashing out and is incapable of love. I will show you this kid is unique. Holding DNA that is above the fray of American misconception and racial stereotype. Let's take a moment to consider what he has endured? One. Unwanted family separation. Two. Extended foster care. Three. Forced relocation. Four. Cultural upheaval.

Now consider what he has done in a short period of time. One. Proven he can adapt. Two. Learned a different set of values and cultural norms. Three. Learned to love and respect two people he was forced to accept as parents. Four. Maintained a positive life attitude in spite of these challenges. Five. excelled in a completely different environment. And six. He never quit.

He has shown all of you in this town who he is; fully transparent, defender of others, respectful to elders, open and optimistic. Yes, he is highly opinionated. He has been helpful to many of you here in this room. He is creative and talented. You've all seen these things from him. Never a foul word expressed in anger unless it was directed at the truth. Never a lie. Never snitching on others. I know these things about him because I put these qualities in him.

Yes, we had a home in a tough neighborhood. But we had a shield of love for each other and friends that protected us from the darker forces that surrounded us. Was it made of vibranium? Hmmm? Maybe, but it was certainly not Captain America shielding us. America was too busy tearing us down, ripping our culture apart, withholding truths from us, lying to us, hating us. So yes, the imperfections of life touched our home as it has touched many of yours. Because this country programmed thiis in many of us.

There's only one heaven and we ain't there yet. In this universe we must try, learn and work and fight our way through the pearly gates using the shield of love. In the end that's all we have. Forgive me for getting a little sappy. Yes, this is personal. But yet there is another injustice about to be rammed down your throats. But why? Dont you wonder where all of this is coming from? Just look across the isle. But before I throw shade on the opposition let me say this.

The evidence is clear. My defendant had no motive and no means to kill his adopted parents. Considering his circumstances, he had that opportunity everyday. The prosecution would have you believe he was just laying in the weeds waiting for his opportunity. A ridiculous assumption as none of you have ever seen a hint of deceit or underhandedness or machiavellian traits from Darnell. Yet he is a killer? Of love? Of life? Of hope? I know you good and honest people of Lincoln, the bedrock of honesty, where the man Abe Lincoln himself proved to you all from right here on this very floor, that honesty, integrity, and common sense are what keep us human. Anger, pride, dishonesty, self absorption and greed are what tear our country and our souls apart. I yield the floor."

Applause from the Darnell side.

Hammering, hammering.

Darnell looked up at his father in awe as he strode back to the table.

- Logan County Courthouse

Part 5

STRATEGY

CHAPTER 23

ON THE STAND

December 27

Amild December winter has yet to open up its can of woop-ass on Central Illinois. All of Lincoln awaits the dump of snow that will shut down farming operations. Anticipation of the winter's annual frosty stretch usually ramps up composting and mulching the top layer of soil to protect it from the freeze.

However, cropland preparation is much less the focus as the chilly swirl of the trial waylaid their work. The distraction had Lincolnites from both camps glued to their radios and televisions, a sickening modern version of the FDR fireside chats of the 1930 and 40s. Family discussions became disagreements leading to arguments as households took sides.

The night air plummeted. Breezes took bites out of the skin like piranha teeth, especially at higher elevations, like on rooftops. Shielded from the cold breezes but not the lowering night temperatures, Percy awaited his 9pm call from inside the rooftop phone booth. Butch Sizemore, FBI SAC Chicago, called in exactly on time. The rooftop phone vibrated.

"Manny's Chicago Pizza."

"We secure?"

"Yea. Any updates?"

"Not sure of relevancy, you'll have to make that call counselor. Don't want to open this door too quickly. Raise suspicions. Also you know he won't allow any of it during the trial. Dirty fuck." Butch said.

"Understand. What you got?"

"So your hunch was spot on. He did have his dick in the midnight mass at the state house when the bill was passed. My sources have him going in the courthouse at 10 pm and leaving after three AM, when they passed the bill. Only floor members were supposed to be allowed in there. Delegate Cindy Owens, a retired FBI agent under me, told me that Red was in a side room with select members on that side of the isle. He had the ears of legacy old farts and large-scale business owners in the house and senate. The speaker allowed him to speak to the entire chamber prior to vote casting."

"The hell?"

"Yea. He went on about moving Illinois forward. How bi-partisan support is critical now more than ever. Both a progressive and fiscally conservative vote will be a win win. Blah blah. How passage of the bill will open up incredible economic opportunities for more people in the state than ever before. Then get this, he zeroed in on Central Illinois, the stomping grounds of Od Abe, as he called it. He talked adnauseam about how that area's history, leading the state in progressive ideas, yada yada. How he guaranteed that it will be the next boom region for the state. How the enrichment of this area will push the state forward economically bringing in trillions of tax dollars over the next few decades. How the bill passage will also bring more federal dollars to the region through specific minority block grant monies as well as federal infrastructure development dollars will come pouring in for decades. How this bill adoption will open the flood gates to this cash reserve the feds are holding for large-scale businesses and infrastructure, healthcare, energy, transportation projects, including the relocation of many federal agency headquarters in DC. And for companies with at least 10% minority ownership, Black or Indian. Saying will be reparations for the ills of the past. How this bill will set well with minority communities of Illinois knowing their children will prosper from its passage."

"I see. But that's a bunch of bullshit. The state and Fed don't have that kind of eminent domain out here at that scale."

"Correct. But they all caved. Passed by 20 votes with a fair amount of the Black Caucus chiming in. Especially those with large business ties. The urban block said fuck that shit."

"How does he know all of this?"

"Obviously he has friends in low places because those fed block grants are not public info yet. They holding it in DC until more legislation is passed on other issues having to do with voting rights, Confederate Civil War heroes names being removed from federal property and PEL Grants minority applications percentages increases. Those will take decades to pass. Multiple presidents."

"The hell?"

"I'm telling you, this thing runs deep Percy. My counterparts in DC government in the Blacks in Government organization and the Black Caucus are buzzing right now about this. Many of them stand to gain. It's like a spreading greed cancer."

"Ok got it. Send me copies of the zoning requests and development proposals submitted to the state for the warehouses, private roads, rail lines, casinos, weather stations, big Pharma labs and corporate headquarters relocation applications?"

"On the way. Closer hold than your nuts, ok?"

"Understand. Keep in my back pocket for emergencies."

"This shit is big Perce. Even the World Wide Catholic Charities organization has submitted major development proposals."

"And you think somehow Darnell is involved?"

"A hunch. Like your sizzle thing but I got nothing solid here about that yet. Sorry. Still the mystery I can't solve."

"Hmm. We will focus on the case and clip around the corners with this other info to test the prosecution. I know McDougle won't allow any of it. But it will put him on notice that we may or may not know something."

"Howzit going? The trial?"

"As expected. One sided. We don't stand a chance in there. We going straight to appeal, no doubt. Get this in front of the supreme court. That's where this other info will surface. We will need much more time for that. Need to get out of this town. The jury is bought and sold. Their Mob roots resurfacing. Another type of cancer. It's spreading to some of the good ones now."

"Damn. But can Darnell withstand the wait on the appeal? He's a kid. He can't do time. Maybe in juvie but he don't need or deserve any of that shit. That could ruin him."

"Understand. We gotta figure this out"

"Anything on the dirty kid yet?"

"Nothing. The fellas are working around the clock. If he's still here, they will find him."

"Clock ticking bro. I'm sending agents down to help with the search."

"Hope it's not too late. So many eating so much dirt here."

"Only money, power and sex can do that my brother."

"Butch, don't blow this shit up down here. Small town. No need to drop a shit storm on their heads over this."

"Roger that. Let it paay out."

"10-4. Out."

December 31

"After only three days of witness testimony, the fireworks are getting more intense in the interracial murder case unfolding in Lincoln. WGN Reporter Desiree Justine continues her coverage this early morning. Good morning Desiree. Sun just peeking up in chilly corn country?"

"Yes, yes it is Merri. And yes the fireworks are on full display at the Lincoln courthouse this week. The trial is moving incredibly fast. Witness testimonies are extremely tense. Councilman Whitaker's crossings are tearing holes in the prosecution's witnesses. However, Whitaker's objections to sustains ratio from Judge McDougle are heavily one sided for the state, causing great frustration for the defense team. One damning testimony by the local Sheriff Gabe Tucker has accused murderer Darnell Whitaker of yielding the murder weapon while running from the scene. The Sheriff says he stopped Whitaker from escaping. Said he was looking to shoot more people so he wrestled the gun away from the teenager, perhaps saving more lives. Other witness say they saw and heard Whitaker acting irrationally that day at a local sandwich shop and at the theater. Some said he scared them with his behavior. They felt threatened."

"A seemingly steep hill for the Chicago defense team to climb wouldn't you say Desiree?"

"The defense will bring witnesses today in what has become a very fast moving and intense trial. At the speed of this trial, some think the defense may rest this afternoon calling for closing arguments soon. With today being December 31st, the trial will take a holiday tomorrow. Reporting live this New Years eve from the Logan County Courthouse for WGN, I'm Desiree Justine.

"Objection your honor! Defense is badgering the witness again! He already answered the question."

"Sustained."

"Let me ask it another way Sheriff Tucker. Did the defendant point the gun at you? Remember, there were multiple eye witnesses at the scene."

"Well he had it up kinda like this."

"Let the record show that the defendant is not demonstrating an action indicating the gun was pointing at him."

"Objection! We don't know the mental state of the defendant at that critical time. He could have been attempting to point the gun at the Sheriff but could not see him clearly because of the sun angle we determined yesterday. You honor we've been through this already. Can we move on?"

"Sustained. Move on Mr. Whitaker."

"So since the defendant did not actually point the gun at you"

"Objection. Asked and answered.. Putting words in his mouth. That's not a question your honor. C'mon!"

"Sustained."

Murmurs from Darnell's side.

Hammering.

"According to your testimony, all of the witnesses who saw what was happening with you and the defendant in the street were all behind the defendant." Percy pushed.

"But he could have turned."

"But he did not."

"Well."

"Also you testified that you wrestled the gun away from him? Correct?"

"Uh yea."

"How much do you weigh sir?'
"Objection! Inmaterial."
"I will allow it. Answer the question Sheriff."
Rumbles from the gallery.
Hammering.
"About 275 giver take."
"So you had to wrestle with this five foot nine inch 155 pound teenager to get the gun away? What kind of fight did he put up sir?"
"Uh well he."
"Objection. What kind is not a qualifier. Sheriff is not a professional wrestler for God's sake."
"Sustained."
"Did he kick and claw at you? Remember Sheriff, the eye-witnesses are here."
"Well no."
"Did he spit on you? Careful sir."
"Uh no."
"Did he try to run away with the gun in hand?"
"Uh no. But he..."
"Not much wrestling going on then was it Sheriff?"
"Well he was actin all crazy like."
"And so you used your police training to deescalate like you told us about your glowing record and qualifications yesterday, right?"
"Well I tried to."
"Thus according to this testimony, you had no reason to wrestle him?"
Hammering hammering hammering!
"Thats all your honor."
"Cross?"
"No your honor."
"Call your next witness."
"Defense calls Darnell Whitaker."

CHAPTER 24

DO I DO

All eyes in the courtroom watched the teen take an unsure walk to the stand. Percy gave him a reassuring wink and mouthed the words, "its okay." After swearing in, McDougle warned the gallery to remain silent and there will be no more outbursts in his court or he will clear the room. He then warned Percy to keep his witness examinations legal and professional. Percy did not respond.

"Objection. Your honor, council's examination of his own son cannot be accepted as normal. There will be all kinds of nuance that the jury will not catch thus giving an unfair advantage. This must not be." Frongello pushed.

"Overruled. Continue counselor but I am warning you. Contempt will not be tolerated in my court. You do understand. Remember your training. Impartiality keeps lawyers out of jail."

"Of course your honor. We understand the situation and so to help matters, we request questioning be conducted by co-lead counsel JC Monroe, if that is ok your honor."

"Suit yourself."

In a grey, very business sleek pant-suit, sporting blood-burgundy pumps, JC Monroe confidently walked to the stand. A mild rumble buzzed from the anti-Darnell side.

Hammering.

"I'm warning you people!"

"Hello Darnell. How are you?"

"Fine thank you."

"Really? How are you managing all of this?"

"Ok, I guess."

"You guess?"

"I spose. Never been through anything like this before."

"No? Wern't you a troublesome teen?"

"No, I don't think so."

"Fighting. Stealing. Cursing. Lying. Playing hooky from school. Idolizing drug dealers and gang bangers?"

"No."

"Hmm. Because that is what the prosecution would have the court believe."

"Objection."

"Sustained. Please Ms. Monroe. Theatrics from you as well? Didn't I teach you better than that?"

"No sir you did not. According to your school disciplinary records I have here as exhibit C, you are correct. You have a total of zero entries for disciplinary actions. Hmm. What about your scholastic record? Let's see Exhibit D. Darnell James Whitaker, Chicago Public School Academic Record and Transcript. Hmm let's see here."

"Objection! Irrelevance."

"I am trying to establish a pattern and dispel the alternate facts the prosecution introduced earlier about my client."

"Overruled."

"Hmm. In Chicago you averaged a 3.6 GPA. Your record from your current Lincoln High School has no disciplinary actions and a 3.7 average for the semester. Hmm. Your Chicago record, which goes back to elementary school. It does indicate you got in trouble in the sixth grade. Do you remember what for?"

"No."

"It says you had comic books in class." Gallery snickered.

Hammering.

"I guess."

"My my. What an egregious offense."

"Objection!"

"Sustained."

"A eggish what?"

"Never mind Darnell. So Darnell, tell the people about your experience coming to Lincoln."

"From the beginning?"

"Absolutely."

"Well when they came to get me."

"You mean Chicago Social Services?"

"Yes. I did not want to come here because I was about to go into 12th grade and I did not see the point."

"Why? Weren't you in a foster home? Didn't you want to get out and have a real adopted family?"

"I mean yes and no. I mean I was actually ok where I was. I loved Mamma Gene and the kids. I was there for a long time. They were my family. I was the big brother."

"Let the record show that Darnell was with the same foster family with Mamma Gene for four years and nine months. Go one please."

"Well when they came to get me I was totally against it. I wasn't going anywhere. I'll said just wait till the end of summer at least. Everything I had was where I was. I didn't know these people and I didn't think they knew me. But the social lady and the police were there and they made me go with them immediately. It was so rushed."

"You were forced?"

"I mean they showed me some papers and said I would go to jail or something if I did not sign them and do what they said."

"Let the record show exhibit E, City of Chicago Adoption Contract stating exactly what the defendant has sated. He could be detained if he did not comply and go with the Wagners immediately. I ask the court is this not coercion? Note his signature. And needing this type of order to pass the city and state newly authorized interracial adoption law, can add collusion?"

"Objection. No proof of this assertion your honor."

"Sustained. Court recorder will strike the last comment from the record. Proceed with caution Ms. Monroe." Red eyeballed her hot pumps and wondered what's under that suit.

"Very well. Continue please Darnell."

"Well I had no choice. I had to go."

"Were you angry?"

"I guess."

"How angry?"

"I didn't want to leave my friends, family, Mamma Gene and Nikki." Maria in the gallery leaning in closer to hear.

"Nikki?"

"Yes. My best friend sense first grade. We did everything together. We were never apart. I have guy friends too but Nikki and I know everything about each other. We mostly like the same things. Ya'no?"

"I understand. And was Nikki troublesome?"

"What?"

"Did she influence you to do things that adults did not like? Did she egg you on to stay? To fight back?"

"Heck no! She was always the voice of reason. The yin to my yang." Maria smiled.

"Ok. Go on."

"She was the one who pushed the hardest for me to go with the new parents. She told me to go become the best I could be then return to Chicago to go to college and then become whatever I want to be. She said Chicago is full of bad things and bad people." He peered over to McDougle. A short stare down. "She said the city will chew me up and spit me out.

She said there is only death in the city if you do not have lots of money. Nikki knows. She understands. She understands everything."

"I see. So you took her advise."

"Yes. She helped me pack up and I was gone. Just like that. They didn't allow me to say goodbye to anyone accept whoever was in the house. It was crazy. I felt rushed."

"Do you understand why that was now?"

"Yes. Because I was tuning 18."

"That's right. Tomorrow."

"Yes. And I would no longer be eligible for adoption. Dad said that mom could not have children and they been wanting me for five years but could not get me because of the laws or something, I guess? But now they could take me so they did. Dad said they were committed to me and did not want to give up on me, ever."

"Let the record show that Mr. Whitaker referred to his adopted parents as Mom and Dad multiple times. Go on."

"Well, I mean they are my mom and dad." He looked over to his father in court. They stared at each other. Percy nodded in affirmation that he is doing good. They know the gallery and judge will interpret it differently. "I mean they were."

"So how did you accept things when you got here?"

"It was a little difficult. These people were strange to me. Talk different, act different, laugh a lot. They have parties all the time, always eating, going places. Funny smells, all kinds of animals everywhere, crops all over. I was, was, was"

"What?"

"Overwhelmed I guess."

"Were you mad. Angry?"

"Not like that. I was just, I don't know, just confused at all of this happening so fast."

"How and when did you begin to settle into all of this?"

"Looking back. I think the first day I arrived I felt like I was drowning and then Maria came up to me and helped me see things better."

"You mean Maria Marmarou?"

"Yes. Her over there." Pointing her out, she stared at him emotionless, awaiting his next words.

"How?"

"She was also sent here like me. We the same age. She been here almost two years from a big city also and knew the deal around here. She began to make things clear to me how people are. What they're like, ya no? She has a way of making the bad seem good. So I listened to her. Then my new parents showed me how awesome they really are. Dad was from Chicago. He was a hooper back in the day."

"Hooper?"

"Basketball player in the city. He convinced me to tryout for the high school team. I did. I made it. And the guys are great. The best players I have ever played with."

The entire team stood in the back of the gallery, smiled and waved.

Hammering.

"Enough of that!"

"Go on."

"Well, everyone I met seemed to be incredible. They either were doing things for me or with me. Showing me things I had never seen. Opening their homes to me. I must have been in at least fifty peoples houses here. Mom and dad know everybody here. Dinners, parties, helping out, hanging out, whatever. Me and Maria explored all kinds of places around here from the lakes to the parks, the rivers, the fair and farms, concerts, ball games and shops, especially the comic book store where Mayor Dez works. Me and him are book heads. He's awesome and knows a lot about the books."

"You mean comic books? For the record."

"Yes. He and I work on saxophone stuff together at the store. He's a killer player."

"Go on please."

"I learned about growing strawberries, sheep, goats, cows, corn, wheat, soy, pigs. I would of never known this stuff if I was in Chicago. I got to shave an Alpaca. And a llama spit on me!

Chuckling.

Hammering.

"So in the short time you were here, you went from anger to happiness?"

"Well I was never angry at anything. This place gave me nothing to be angry about."

"What about your biological father and mother? Didn't you want them in your life?"

"Of course I did but it seemed like that wasn't gonna happen. My mom in Chicago is in the hospital and cannot leave yet. Nikki gives me reports."

"And what about your father? That man over there? Aren't you angry at him?"

"I was when I was like 12 or 13. I got use to him not being there. There was so much going on at Mamma G's that she never let me slip into that darkness mode. Mamma G would try to talk to me about my father but I couldn't hear that then. I was busy with everything else. Every time his name came up at the house, I would remember back to that night he left and I did not want to remember that."

"Why not?"

"It was ugly."

"How so?"

"My mom was really drunk and high and stuff one night. My dad came home from working his night job after being in college all day, to find her there like that. They were yelling then they started fighting."

"Did you see that?"

"Yes."

"How much of it did you see?"

"All of it. After my dad came in my room to see if I was sleeping, he went into his bedroom. I got up to give him a hug and tell him what I did that day, but I heard him yelling at my mom about the drugs. I watched everything from the door. They did not see me cuz they were going at it hard. My mom was crazy on drugs and my dad tried to stop her but she was crazy-eyed. She said she would kill him. I was so scared. I froze. Dad tried to stop her but he had to hit her to slow her down. It was, was horrible."

Tears uncontrollably rolled down Maria's face. She shook in her chair. She did not know about this. Other sobs and sniffles from the gallery on both sides.

Hammering

"Do we need a recess people?"

"Darnell? Do you want to stop now?"

"No, I'm good."

"You had every right to be angry at your father."

"Not really. I was angry at my mother. He told her to stop over and over. Every month she would have a bad trip he had to take care of her mess. And he had two jobs. She didn't even work! But she was a great mom to me. The best." He sniffed.

"If we can continue, please tell the court what happened the day of the murders here.

"We were having a good day. We got chili and sandwiches at Deep Roots Café and were going to the movies like we usually do on Sunday afternoon."

"Do you recall saying somethings that were offensive to others?"

"What all those people said who came up here to talk about me is not true. When I said I would shoot racists in the head with silver bullets, I was talking about the silver bullets of Truth that the Silver Surfer uses. He was an astronomer from the planet Zenn-La. A peaceful place. But he was sent to earth after loosing his wife to Galactus and Surfer became his intergalactic servant. Galactus did not let him go home but assigned him to Earth. He shieded him insive andgave him a flying board that he trasitted fromplanetto planet doing things for Galactus. But he learned to love Earth the most but he hated the bad people here so he did things to them to make them better people. He used the mind-changing silver bullets to shoot into bad peoples heads who are not thinking right. People with bad thoughts and stuff. Even crooks and robbers. Those silver bullets are what keeps earth from falling into chaos. But he always found more bad people and got madder at the humans for being so stupid and mean."

"Let the court show that Silver Surfer is a comic book character. Do you have a gun?"

"No!"

"Have you ever shot a gun?"

"No."

"Have you ever held or been in the presence of a gun?"

"Yes, Dad has two hunting rifles in the gun locker at home. He opened it up one time to show me. He said we would go deer hunting in the winter. I said I didn't want to go hunting. That it's wrong to kill deer for fun. He said we would eat the meat and I said that is gross and I wouldn't go. We never talked about it again."

"Did you hold the rifle?"

"No. He didn't take it out the locker."

"Were there other guns in the locker?"

"I don't know. There were green boxes and black smaller cases and stuff."

"Do you know where he kept the key?"

"It is a combination lock like a school locker."

"Do you know the combination?"

"No."

"Please continue with your story of that horrible day. If you cannot finish it's ok."

"Um, we were eating lunch talking about what the movie is supposed to be about. I thought it was a stupid idea for a movie. How black people always have stupid parts in movies or they are made to look bad or the first to die. I don't go to those type of movies. But mom thought it was a comedy. I was trying to tell her that it is a racist theme. A white kid steals the only black scholarship to Harvard in Los Angeles by changing his skin color to brown with tanning pills and wears an afro wig? And the people at Harvard believed him? C'mon! That's ridiculous and insulting to all the smart black people out there who want to get into Harvard or other big colleges?"

"I see your point."

Gallery noise increasd with agreement and disagreement.

"Objection."

Hammering.

"Sustained."

Groaning.

Hammering.

"Continue please."

"Well, people heard us talking and started saying mean things to me. Dad tried to defend me but they called him names too. I was mad at them people for being mean to us. For nothing!"

"And then what happened?"

"Then as we were leaving the theater, another guy was really aggressive towards us. So dad took us through the alley cut next to the theater because our car was parked on Pulaski and this guy was following us and yelling at us."

"Did you feel threatened?"

"Heck yea. I was a little scared cuz he was acting like a crazy dude."

"Please tell the court what happen next."

"We turned into the alley and then turned to the part where you can go out to Polaski street by the the Alley-Bi Saloon. That's when this drunk dude pulled a gun on us trying to rob us. Said he wanted our wallets. Dad tried to talk him out of it when the dude said he recognized mom and dad from the Kroger store. I didn't know what he was talking about. Then he was saying crazy stuff about how he already killed Mr. Frys."

"Let the record state Mr. Frys was the manager of the Kroger who died along with his pregnant wife in a suspicious house fire, according to Lincoln Fire Department recently."

"He said he killed Mrs. Martins."

"Let the record state that Mrs. Martins is Ruthy Martins who has come up missing recently. Go on Darnell."

"And he said he killed Mr. Mansfields and a bunch of babies."

"Let the record also state that Mr. Mansfields was recently killed along with several other people and children including several babies in an explosion at the day care center recently. Go on."

"Objection. Your honor the witness is clearly trying to exonerate himself and implicate a fictional comic book character."

"I will allow but Mr. Whitaker, you cannot use anyones name in this portion of your testimony if it accuses or implicates. Just answer the questions."

"Go on."

"Well he said he was looking for us and now he found us and he can clean the slate or something like that. His hand was shaking and he pointed the gun at dad. Dad went for the gun and it went off. Mom got hit in the face. Dad was struggling with the dude and the gun went off again. Dad got hit and he went down."

"What did you do?"

"I was on the ground with mom. I picked up a piece of metal pipe and smashed his knee. He dropped the gun and went down. I picked up the gun and pointed it at him. He started laughing at me calling me ugly racist names and stuff. He dared me to shoot. Said I was too stupid. He called me a monkey and stuff. I turned and fired the gun aiming past him intentionally to scare him. Then this cook came out of Ally-Bis and was freaking out. I told him that guy shot my parents. The shooter dude said he didn't shoot them but I did! Said a white boy would never kill two white people. I tried to tell the cook what happened. When I looked back at the shooter he was gone. I was panicking. I jumped up to go after him. I didn't know which way he ran out of the alley. Left or right. I ran left back to Kickapoo Street but he was not there. He must have run the other way out the alley where all the trash is, towards Chicago Street. That's when the Sheriff happen to be right there. I fell on the ground scared. He pulled out his gun and told me to drop the pistol so I did. I tried to tell him what happened but I couldn't hardly speak. He helped me into the police car and I blacked out. Next thing I know I woke up in a jail cell."

"Do you have anything more to add?"

"No ma'am."

"Darnell do you recognize this person?" She showed him a mug shot of Russell Smerker.

"I think so."

"Where have you seen him? Is he the one who shot your parents?"

"Yea. That definitely could be him. The guy had on this floppy brim hat that kinda covered his face. But that could be him."

"Objection. The defendant is trying to tie an innocent person to this horrible crime. This can do irrefutable harm to this person if this gets out. No positive ID. I ask that it not be entered into record." Fronngello stood in a mild panick.

"Sustained. Enough of that Ms. Monroe."

"I think that's him. He's the killer! That's him!"

"Let the record state that the defendant identified Russell Smerkers."

"Objection! Your honor!

"Your honor, my client just placed the actual suspect at the scene."

"No he did not counselor. He cannot positively say that is him so this will not be entered into evidence. Move on I said. The jury will strike that portion of the testimony."

"But…"

"I said move on counselor."

"No more questions."

"Prosecution, cross?"

"Your honor. We have seen and heard the skills and intellectual gifts this killer has. He is a cunning bright and masterful story teller, raised on comic books and fantasy stories as we have heard. Comic books ladies and gentlemen. Really? And counselor talks about us being in another universe? How far out can one get? Which side is the alternate universe I ask? I fear that if I go down this road with him, we will be here for another hour of epic story telling from Planet Whitaker. Now a later interjection of a possible suspect? C'mon. Ladies and gentlemen of the jury, you are seeing some of the best witness coaching known to the lawyering field. We all here know what happened. Testimony after testimony proved it.

"Objection. Your honor prosecution is making a speech and not cross examining the witness."

"If you have no further questions for the witness may be excused."

"That is all your honor." Frongello smugly went back to his binder pulling out papers for closing arguments.

"Defense rests your honor." Percy rose to announce.

"Let's take a 15 minute break. Bailiff, remand the prisoner to the court holding cell. We will reconvene for closings in 15 minutes. I want to see both counselors right here, now!"

Percy and Frongello approached the bench.

"Let me say this one more time. We have a tinder box in here. I suggest you two do your god-damnedest to not light no fucking fuse in my court. You get these arguments in and out and do not riel these locals up. Am I clear?"

"But your honor, there are clear distinctions here that neither sides like. Nothing short of a quick thank you will please this group. They're looking for blood." Percy forced at McDougle.

"Well Mr. Whitaker, either you cut your wrists open for these zombies or zip up your petticoat. Because if you light this powered keg, there'll be hell to pay. Am I clear.?"

"Yes your honor."

The courtroom mostly cleared for recess as the crowd headed to the toilets and vending machines. TV news reporters scrambled outside to shoot taped stand-ups or live hits. Newspaper journalists raced for the wall phones to file stories before deadline.

The two counselors moved past the judges bench to the back hall for the attorney lavatories.

"Hey Percy can I talk to you?"

CHAPTER 25

HOLIDAY BREAK

The usually solemn hallowed halls of the Logan County Courthouse became loud aggressive sounding tunnels full of the cries of desperate furry by creatures trying to escape, come in, or stand their ground. All bumping into each other and not liking the physical contact. Officers Bruce Butler and Ryan Sullivan headed off potential eruptions between nose to nose debaters. The officers picked out potential known trouble makers who may have slipped through the first round of entries. Anyone who exits the building cannot re-enter and no new entries from the line are allowed in.

Maria was in the face of a short fat greasy looking dude with balding stringy weeds for hair. She's was giving him the business about Darnell's innocence but he is all in on guilty. Every part of the main hall and corridors were full of loud debaters.

A scream from a woman down one corridor was followed by a booming crash. Butler and Sullivan pushed through the crowd to see what's the fracas. They found two large woman tussling on top of eachother on a smashed bench. One large barefooted woman in a flowery dress had her hands clamped around the throat of the other large barefooted woman in a flowery dress. The one on top had the other pinned flat on the smashed wooden bench next to a water fountain. The officers peeled the refrigerators apart at their own peril. The four tussled, flailed and stumbled across the floor. Shoeless, red faced and wild haired, the puffing bulls faced off with their fists up. Officer Butler made a move to separate them further. The women exploded into a furious pinwheel of haymakers. Officer Sullivan got clocked on the top of his head trying to push them apart. His face buried in the DDD sized bosom of one of the rhinos. He caught another shot to the back of his neck. Butler clamped one of the tanks in a half Nelson, shoving her away from the dancing couple of Sullivan and his big sweaty dance partner. They pushed the two tractors in opposite directions. Thcy shoved the sliding growling floral grizzly bears across the marble floors in their stocking feet. One into the ladies room, the other out of the nearest emergency exit.

Percy and Frongello were shielded from the commotion in the back hall, headed to the Mens room. Frongello in-front of Percy, nothing said. Before entering the restroom, Frongello stopped and turned.

"Hey Perce. Can we talk?"

"I got nothing to talk about."

"Look Perce, we're attorneys. We deal right? It's what we do. Aren't you ready to make a deal yet? You see what's going on right now don't you?"

"Yea I see. But I'm not ready to make a deal right now."

"Be smart Percy. You see what's happening?"

They entered the restroom, headed straight to the urinals. Percy put a urinal between the two. They unzipped.

"What's going on is this coffee coming out of me after four hours of your bullshit Frong."

"Well my roots in law run deep and long."

"So you think. Deep in the crap pool. You have no idea about my roots and my length."

Frongello stepped back a half step from the urinal still his stream reached the bowl.

"Yea but my reach is further than you think."

Percy stepped back a half step behind Frongello, still hitting the bowl.

"You underestimate me counselor. You know nothing about me."

Frongello backed up another half step still hitting the bowl.

"Oh I know you alright." Frongello stepped back a half step further behind percy. "I know what you got going on down South, Mr. Save the Day Superman of the Hood. But what is that going to get you today? You know where the real lawyering is. It's back here where the longest deepest tentacles reside."

Percy stepped back another half step, still hitting the back of the urinal with his stream.

"Yea I know. Sure I get it. But you haven't seen half of what I can do."

Frongello slid back a little further barely reaching the bowl.

"Ok cowboy. You think your roots run deep? You don't know who you are mess'in with. Why do you think you can do this Percy?"

Frongello's stream began to droop, hitting the floor between him and the urinal. Percy stepped forward to shake it off inside the bowl. Forngello went to the sink.

"Faith my good man. Faith."

"Faith? Are you kidding me right now? You litigating on faith Percy? We're lawyers Percy. Leave all that alternate universe great omnipotent blah blah blah to these mortals, the people, that's their thing. We're lawyers not priests. We deal in reality. We deal in winning. What are you dealing in? Some hocus pocus bullshit?"

Percy washed his hands and wet toweled his face.

"I deal in people. I'm in the people business Frong. I don't know what kind of fantasy you are living in but I lawyer for people. My people. And my people give me faith. And yes, I have faith in my people. That bullshit you believe in is going to get you burnt or worse." Percy dried his hands and face then headed to the door.

"Suit yourself counselor. You know what the penalty is going to be right? You wanna do that to your boy? Even waiting a year in lock up for appeal will kill him."

"I'm fully aware."

"Sorry about your son. He was a great kid. I know he's special. I totally get it. But if you are willing to sacrifice him, that's on you counselor."

"Look here Frong, if it takes my life to bring down you people, it won't be vengeance for my son, it will be vengeance for the people of Illinois. You and your people come here tearing up the fabric of this country with your criminal activities, extortion, drugs, murder and other non-human insanities. It's so old Frongello, like you. You don't care about the shit you leave in your wake. You represent the worse of us. I represent the best of people. Yea, if I lose my son because of this, trust me, you will not have seen the last of me. Yea it will be personal then. And that faith I'm talking about, will rain hell fire down on your entire Outfit with the furry of Gideon. See you inside counselor."

Frongello looked at his reflection in the mirror as he watched Percy walk out the door.

"…and so I say to you ladies and gentlemen of the jury, we have demonstrated to your common sense's that a seemingly bright and articulate young man who has been suppressing his hidden anger from being ripped away from his comfortable yet sinister upbringing, finally performed the perfect crime. No witnesses, he thought. No outward displays of hate, so he thought. Let's not forget how he slipped with an outburst of his true colors towards our coveted Judge McDougle at a public event. Showing in full color his dark side. We all know when evil lurks within, it soon come. Yes, it soon come. And how tragic it came that day.

The day Lincoln lost its most precious citizens. With the recent passing of Mr. Robert Todd Lincoln Beckwith, our last descendant of Lincoln was ripped from U.S. history! Taken by the selfish rage of a black sociopath that our dear Elizabeth's great great great grand father of freedom and emancipation lived and died to free! He too was taken in a selfish jealous rage. Why? We can only grieve again for our beloved Lincoln. Our great daughter is gone by the hands of some petty disillusion, a disconnected foster kid from the city. A kid angry at his selfish father who left him for the streets so he can make money on the backs of the poor?

And we are surprised at this outcome? No! We the people of this great town of Old Honest Abe are outraged! You should not sit there and be hoodwinked by all of this South Side slick gamesmanship and word twisting. You are the common folk, the real America. The common sense folk that make this great American engine run. But, like my lovely Italian mother would say, when there is fly in the soup, holly cannoli! So there is only one logical verdict here. An eye for an eye as we are taught by our foundational christian national patriotic ethics; a life for a life.

That is justice. And we are a just nation; a nation of laws; a nation of rules, and ethics, and not this lawless behavior from ghetto hoodlums. So this is about losing his comic books! Really? If all it takes is a comic book to inspire murder of your parents, a not guilty verdict means he is free to kill again and again. Right here in Lincoln. For what? No ice in his pineapple soda? Are you kidding me? You are the people of the land. You are the heart and soul of this nation. I ask you to use the superior gift of intelligence God has bestowed upon you chosen ones to feed and nourish this nation and find Darnell Whitaker guilty of two counts of murder in the first degree. The prosecution rests your Honor. I yield the floor."

"Counselor, your closing please." McDougle shifted in his seat.

"Murder for comics? Wow. I want to apologize to you all. I would like to ask for your forgiveness. Please forgive the insults that were just thrust upon all of you. To the people of this gallery who are here to express their right to assemble, you have just been assaulted by councilman Frongello in a way I have never heard. He insults your intelligence and common senses by weaving this thin layer of cheese cloth over your heads, how insulting.

Yes, these were two murders of tragic proportion. So much has been lost. We know this. We all feel it. But to try and find a killer by fabricating a back story and manipulating your good senses is incredible. Your eyes see and your ears hear. But the prosecution says you are deaf dumb and blind. You have seen and heard my client, and yes my son is my client. You've seen him at his best and his worse. And none of his behaviors demonstrated the signs of a suppressed killer. Do you actually think Chuck and Liz spent five years studying their perfect child to miss one small detail? Oh by the way, he is a sociopathic killer? A blatant insult to the Wagners' and your collective intelligences'.

And your beloved judge here today. The man who facilitated the adoption. You actually think a man of his brilliance and stature would risk his reputation by recommending a killer to his own cousin? C'mon people. Really? None of you here today who know Darnell, have ever heard him fabricate a story. If he spoke of fiction, it was about the characters of his readings, yes comics. His hero's are defenders of the common man. Not the crazed villains who seek to destroy.

Who are they? We heard about Silver Surfer. The outcast who wants to protect humans from their bad intentions. Black Panther. The king of an advanced African nation who fights to protect his culture. Luke Cage, an inner-city super hero who goes after inner-city bad guys, like the mob, to correct wrongs. There's Black Lightening. A former school teacher in the inner city who began intervening in student's violent behaviors, to become the defender of the poor and underprivileged. There's Blade, the vampire exterminator. Who likes vampires? There's Misty Knight, a highly skilled female detective solving crimes. There's Vixen, a female African crime fighter given the powers of the animals. There is the Falcon who replaced Captain America. Captain America my good people. Nuff said about that.

There are so many more that this young man is incredibly knowledgable of. But what's the common thread here? If you are not as tuned into these characters, myself included, then I'll spell it out for you. They are all heroes who fight for good! For your good ladies and gentlemen; protecting not destroying. There are many destructive villains in the comic world. Mind you that the comic book industry is a multi-billion dollar industry. With world-wide appeal to millions and millions of people of all ages, genders, and races. So before you brush the comic literature aside, please consider these facts.

There are learned people among you here who understand the value of literature. You understand the critical role reading plays in young brain development. Of course you are what you eat. This young man is not a school teacher or college professor, yet. But he is unknowingly training his mind to research through words and not hearsay. He must have read more than 2000 comic books in his life, probably more.

You heard from his teachers and school counselors, and your neighbors speaking on his behalf; no sociopath here. So consider the insult that was just laid upon you by the prosecution. Now, as for the murders; the only witness besides Darnell was the cook from Alley-Bi. But you saw the prosecution discredit him because of his previous criminal record, incarceration and lying in court on other occasions. But he was there. And he gave similar testimony to the description of the real perpetrator. Darnell spoken to this man before nor after the murders. How could their stories be so similar?

So you tell me, tell yourselves, tell your community what makes sense to your collective intelligence's? The insults of nonsense from that side or the understanding of reason from this side. I'm not looking for your sympathy because I am his father. I am seeking justice on behalf of my client who was so obviously wrongly accused of an act he could not have possibly committed, even on his worse day. You know who you are and who you must live with from this day forward. I ask you to do the right thing and free Darnell from this wrongful accusation. I thank you for your service. I yield the floor."

McDougle hammered for attention. "The jury will be remanded to your quarters for deliberation. You will have no outside contact until your decision is final. Take all the time you need. Since today is December 31st, tomorrow is a holiday. If you do not reach a decision today, we will reconvene after the holiday whenever you have rendered your decision. Take all the time you need. Take the prisoner back to the cell. Good luck and may God bless your decision. This court is at recess."

Hammer.

- It's hit or miss now

CHAPTER 26

WORD IS IN

8:45 PM New Years Eve

We now go live to Logan County where there is breaking news on the Darnell Whitaker double murder case."

"This is Desire Justine from the Logan County Court House where closing arguments for the Lincoln murder trial of Darnell Whitaker have just concluded around 5:30 this evening. Though it is dark now, as you can see behind me, flood lights are illuminating the Logan County Courthouse grounds due to the high volume of people out here still protesting into the night. These people would normally be celebrating New Year's Eve now but it seems the majority of this small town is out here still protesting into the night. Many awaiting to celebrate a decision in their favor. The citizens here are so connected to this case that they are acting as if the decision, which ever way it goes, will be a personal indictment on their way of life and on their town. With the look of this crowd, I don't think they are going anywhere anytime soon. The jury is deliberating now, making the final decision on the fate of the adopted Chicago teenager, Darnell Whitaker, in what has been an incredibly rapid case. We are trying to find an Illinois murder trial that has ever ended so quickly, and so far, this one is at the top.

Both attorneys made powerful closing arguments. Prosecutor Frongello claiming that accused murderer, seventeen year old Darnell Whitaker, is actually a sociopath who has been tactfully planning this murder since being reluctantly and rapidly pulled from his foster home in Chicago earlier this year, and immediately driven to Lincoln to live with new parents. Of course as you know, Darnell is the first black child in the state to be adopted by a white family. The law disallowing these types adoptions was over-turned by an emergency session in the state house and senate earlier this year and Darnell Whitaker was the first black child adopted under the new law.

With me now is prosecuting attorney Robert Frongello. Sir, thank you for taking the time to speak to our audience. Can you tell us how you think your side did today convincing the jury that Darnell Whitaker is a sociopath who cleverly plotted this horrible murder of his adopted parents?"

"It became increasingly clear after local witness after witness testified that he exhibited these signs."

"What signs?"

"Little indicators that he was displeased with his surroundings. He even said it himself that he was angry that he was forcefully pulled out of his loving home in Chicago to come here to the middle of corn country. I can only imagine the pain and suffering this kid must have endured. Family uprooting can be a mental trigger for an advanced mind to fall into a deep depression and feeling of hopelessness. It is a sad state of affairs in our country today. But it has become very common in many of the underclass communities in our cities. Circumstances like he had suffered can shape his vulnerable mentality into a revengeful mindset. If this thing goes the way we believe it will go, the state needs to bare some of the responsibility for this awful situation. They rushed him through a brand new system. A system that had not been fully fleshed out. I mean you can't just throw these type of children into just any home and expect it to go all Mayberry RFD."

"But Mr. Whitaker told how he changed since being here, how he loves it so much. How his new parents actually became the parents he called mom and dad."

"Well these type babies…"

"What type babies sir?"

"These ghetto children. Born and raised in the ghetto. They are so inundated with social messages counter to what the good people in places like this are accustomed to. So he had great training and preparation for pulling off a cunning attack like this. We saw how smart he is. Hell, he reads more comic books than I read law books. Ha ha."

"But there is no evidence that he brought any ugliness from the South Side of Chicago here to Lincoln.""

"Not to the suckers he grifted. Oh, make no mistake. Mr. Darnell Whitaker is a cunning lad. The witnesses all testified to that. I am sure the people of this great and historic town will not let his ghetto become Lincoln's Ghetto."

"And there you have it. Reporting live from the Logan County Court House in Lincoln Illinois, I'm Desiree Justine. Back to you in Chicago."

"Order up! Rueben with Russian, fries, and diet Co-Cola."

"That's me!" Yuri popped up from the table with Percy, JC and Barbara at a packed-in Roots Cafe across from the court house.

"This place normally closes at eight but business is booming! They are preparing for the long haul tonight." Yuri said as he blew bubble fizz from the top of his coke.

"I hate this part the most babe. I hate this part of the job. This part of life. Waiting on someones fate, especially this. Oh my God babe. I'm so scared."

"I know." Percy put his arm around JC.

"How are you babe?" She asked.

"Not good either."

"You not feeling your closing argument?"

"I'm not feeling how uncertain Darnell is feeling right now. I feel him. I feel his angst."

"He did everything perfectly. Just as we rehearsed. You crushed the close. They gotta come back hung. This could take days. Those women are fighters right?" Yuri arranged his plate of fries and drippy rueben.

"Yea. But they have something we don't." Barbara jumped in.

"What's that?" Percy looked to Barbara sideways.

"The influence of community. All them dudes on that jury know all those women. They gonna influence them, maybe even threaten them. Who knows what ties they all have to each other. Could be farming relations, church, school, civic, whatever. This is a real small town ya'no. They could cave as easily as they could decide to endure a long argument. Hell, their husbands may have already influenced the hell out of them."

"At least Maria is with him," Yuri picked at his fries, not really hungry.

"Yea. One good thing about this place. The jail is empty and it is right next door. Bruce will watch over him." Percy helped Yuri with his fries.

"Still no word from Booker and the team?"

"Nothing. He's scheduled to call in tonight at 9 on the roof."

"Percy, how do you know Officer Bruce Butler again?" Yuri wiped Russian dressing from his mouth, tossing his tie over his shoulder.

"He and I were on a job in Puerto Rico not long ago. I was researching a drug trafficking case there and he came down with me from the city as my personal aid. He's fluent in Spanish and he was a Marine enforcement enforcement officer once and is a former Marine Corp Gunney. He was my dawg down there. A bad hurricane had just passed over the island and then an earthquake hit Ponce when I was there gathering information and evidence from Customs Marine Enforcement officers. We were in a small building across from the historic U.S. Custom House, close to the shoreline. The hurricane saturated the ground then the earthquake came quick. The building shook so violently, it began to collapse on us. The building was old and it just started to break apart. The ground was saturated. The floor and walls started to split open underneath and around us. We thought the roof was going to cave. All doors were bent and jammed shut. Windows had bars on them. Bruce was outside in the car waiting. He rammed the car into the building, breaking a hole in the wall. The roof started to cave. Water was pouring in. It was chaos. He snatched my ass outta there in a quick. Bruce is solid. He came back and joined the Chicago PD, then took the gig down here in Lincoln. He had enough of the city shit. He's gonna be mayor here. Mark my words."

"Damn!" Russian sauce blob slid down Yuri's shirt, unnoticed by him.

"Well, well, well. Team South Side. Ready to deal now?" Frongello walked up with a meatball sandwich and fries on a tray. "I may be open to Man 2. Irrational spur of the moment act. Hmm. Let's see. What about the gun? That makes it intentional. Maybe I go Man 2 parole after 20. Keep him off the painkiller."

"Jesus. He'll be almost 40 for God's sake." Yuri stood in protest to Frongello's offer.

"We can request Joliet. You can cruise Route 66 straight there on the weekends keep tabs on your boy. See how the animals are treating him. After all, tomorrow he's a man. No juvie for him. McDougle is a heartless bastard."

"Man 2 and 10?" JC asked.

"Um, let me think. You gonna lay off the Outfit?"

"You know I can't do that." She stared him down anticipating a vile response.

"Hmm. Well no and hell no. Man one. Let McDougle have him."

Percy lunged at him. "You son of a bitch!" The meatball sub and fries went up in a a twirl. Barbara and JC pulled them apart. Frongello smiled a cheshire grin, straightening his tie.

"You can take Nigs out of the ghetto but you can't take the ghetto out the Nigs," Frongello laughed and walked out of the small sandwich shop grinning. JC and Barbara restrained Percy from following him.

Suddenly the glass door of Roots flew open with a bang. A hysterical woman bounded inside in a panic.

"They back! They back! The jury is back! Come quick if you wanna get back in there. Hurry!"

"What? It's nine o'clock!"

CHAPTER 27

POP THE CORK

Happy New Year!! 1983

"Driving that train, high on cocaine
Casey Jones you better watch your speed
Trouble ahead, trouble behind
And you know that notion just crossed my mind
This old engine makes it on time
Leaves Central Station about a quarter to nine
Hits River Junction at seventeen to
At a quarter to ten you know it's traveling again
Driving that train, high on cocaine"

Pop pop pop! No waiting for mid-night. Champagne corks popping kicked off early and often at the Old Mill. Cork cracking over the Grateful Dead's song filled the odd and rustic bar full of New Year's celebrators. Locals who were not at the court, slobbered all over each other, celebrating another go-round of the sun. Lincoln's best drinkers never pass up this anxiously awaited night each year at the Mill. The best of the lushes pile in the old Dutch Mill house of freaks and oddities like no other day of the year.

On this night, in this place, the area pros knew that the long-time owner Eleanor, celebrated with the town zombies, bootleggers, sleazy politicians, mob wannabes, and farm swillers, looping for the cheap and easy. Eleanor already had a stable of farm lady lonely's' ready to work the New Year's gaggle. She gets her cut for any trim sold. The old barracks side of the Mill comes in handy for this annual event. Local gals who play this game range from 17-65 years old. They flock into the Mill on this grand evening from surrounding towns like Burton View, Elkton, Fogerty, Evans, Bell, Lawndale, Beason, Waynesville, Clinton and Atlanta. They show up like clockwork every 12/31 for the possible man catch or paid pooty-pop. For them, the liquor, music and chicken cheese snacks are free. The men pay double but don't give two shakes-a-shit cuz it's New Years Baby!

Many show up for an early start around 7:30. By 9pm the 500-pound stuffed cow in the middle of the dance floor has one dude with his head buried deep in the cows' lubed up anus, bobbin for cans of Floyds IPA brew, while a bouncy boobed young filly rode on the cows' back. The noise, deafening. The smoke smoke, gagging.

One guy slow danced with the armor suited mannequin in the corner of the entrance lobby. He was french kissing it's metal helmet's ear hole. A big breasted squealer stuffed jello shots in her cleavage taking on all comers. Bullets in the lobby barrel now have Vietnam era hand grenades, smoke canisters and land mine mortars in it. To say it is a hellish den would be kind.

Twin cow girls enticed the dudes by carrying two bottles of cheap champagne and wearing cow poke hats, boots, tiny leather vests, and chaps with a thong. Whoever slaps their cheeks and can leave a hand print gets to chug from one of their bottles of bubbly. The girls are quick to bend over for a wack.

Men in expensive suits with untucked fully unbuttoned shirts, clinked glasses to celebrate just standing there or whatever. Overall-wearing farm boys not wearing shirts, because their experience knows the place gets hot as a convection oven on high. They offer their sweaty shoulders and backs for the girls to rub.

Eleanor the owner, walked around topping off glasses, amping things up. She started stupid sexy games for prizes on the spot. Like the guy who can hold his crotch with two hands while drinking from a bubbly bottle held with his teeth standing on one foot. His prize is an unlimited chug from a fresh open bottle of Grand Patron. Women race-walk around the cow-centered dance floor, squeezing a champagne bottle between their upper thighs. Most laps in one minute without dropping the bottle gets to sodomize the cow with the bottle still between their legs while guys pour jello shots down her throat. A naked male mannequin lying on its back on the bar has a Champagne bottle in its crotch with a straw in it set up for a round of :60 second sucking.

Needless to say, every one is lit up like Christmas trees on fire. The big event at 11:59pm is what they all await. Once pickled, they all go outside in the cold with 60 seconds left in the old year and they all huddle underneath a giant pair of horse testicles suspended above the front door. The massive testies are a pair of giant beige color balloons with hay glued all over them and filled with hot water. At the stroke of midnight the balls were shot with a 12-gauge shotgun. They explod the hot wash down on everyone giving a refreshing splash of what they call, a New Year's Horse Ball Sweat Rinse. As legend has it, the water from the fruit of the horse will cleanse their inequities from the past year. Yea, ok. They run back inside hooting and hollering, loading up for next ball rinse each hour to honor all of the American time zones. A local superstition Eleanor made up 10 years ago to attract this heathen's den mess. Claims it came from the old country gave it legitimacy.

The only non-white patrons in the pit of ridiculous are two tall sexy Asian women wearing matching low-cut black gowns. Between them doing the worm hula sandwich dance, the Deacon. Sucking vodka from two long flexible straws stuffed down the bosom of each girls low cut dress, connected to a short pint bottle of Popov nestled deep in their wombs. He calls it, his crotch tonic.

With arms around Mikko and Tikko, Deacon saw Russell slumped in a dark corner at the end of the long bar. Deacon brought the girls over to him with fresh champagne bottles. He offered Russell a drink of bubbly but he shrugged it off in his darkness. Deacon introduced the girls. They livened Russell up a bit. He loosened as Deacon offered him a slurp from the crotch straws. They fed him chicken and cheese with vodka and champagne back. At midnight they ran out and get horse balled, then back in. By 4 am Deacon persuaded Russell to go back to the hotel with him and the girls for a four-banger, as he called it. They taxied back to Motel 7.

"Hey, aren't you the guy who got our cash at the church poker table?" The cab driver started the meter.

"Well ain't God good. What you doing out here at four in the moaning? Ain't you got church or sumptim in the morning? Start your year off with a blessing?"

"Hey it's New Years. Always good money this time comin out the Mill. You like that place?" The cabby with the salt and pepper short afro looked in his mirror at the foursome crowded the back.

"Well I just want my lovelies to have a good time. Nothin else goin on in this dish."

"I wanna thank you for letting me get my money back at the table. That was real nice of you."

"No thang but a chicken wang."

"Here's my card. Anytime you need a lift, call direct, not through dispatch. Ask for Curtis, Curtis Abernathy. Anywhere, anytime. My man."

"Awe ain't you just the sweetest."

"Hey you or your buddy there need a pair of shoes? I got these Stacey Adams wing tips. Nice ones. Only thirty bucks for you. Go for ninety-five in the store. But they size 13."

"13!! Lawd! Don't say that too loud in front of my babies here. They know you a 13 they drop me like a bad habit. They on me cuz I got the black dragon. If they know you a 13, they be callin me Pee Wee Herman. Shhhhhh. No thanks."

"Ha! You crazy man! How about your boy there?"

"No. He's too tipsy smashed. He'll probably try to put them on his hands for gloves."

"Ok. Motel 7. Y'all have a good'n, ya hear?"

"What I owe you big boy?"

"Not a note. Pay back for the other day."

"Lord gonna bless you twice as nice this new year. See ya out there trunk."

"Trunk?"

"Like a tree. HAA!!"

The four stammered to the room. Russell so drunk he could hardly stand. He hung on the girls, pawed them like a kitty. They giggled at him and helped him get comfortable in the room.

"You girls take care of him. I'm gonna get some ice and coke for the vodka."

With his room on the first floor, Deacon was stuck in drunken thought trying to decide to take the steps or elevator to the fourth floor where the S.S. crew's rooms were to let them know about Russell. He decided to call them from the front desk, while in search of the ice machine. Seeing the vending machine, he tried to shake out some Fritos. Drunk and stammering, he grabbed his pockets for cigarettes and matches. Seeing a Latina housekeeper setting up her towel cart, he asked her for extra towels and a light. His goofiness and lankiness accentuated by his drunkenness.

"Holahola my senoroomamita. Me needo extro blankettos for me Tikos and Mikkos. You gotto fuego?" Bending over her shortness trying to read her name tag with cigaretter barely stuck to his lips.

"Yannci? Such a lovely Mexican numero." She giggled.

Like a squirrel, his attention diverted to the front desk.

"Damn. Who was I spose to call? Hey Yampita my sweet. Do you have quarters for the snack machine?"

She smiled and pushed her cart down the hall.

"Such lovely pcoples. Specially those black beans and hot tamales."

Dialing Bookers' room number from the front desk phone, he swallowed an almost vomit. "C'mon fat ass wake up!"

"Who is it?"

"My Bootiful nigga roe. Top of the merging to yag guberner."

"Deac what the fuck you want? You drunk? Git the fak off my phone fool. You know what time it is?"

"Do you know what time it is? Tell me do ya know? Do ya do ya know? Put your goochi watch on and sancraize yer clock and let's rock!"

"What the fak are you babbling about? What the hell do you want?"

"I didn't know you knew Rare Essence?"

"What?"

"It's not what I want cuz I gots what you need. Feel me bozo?"

"I'm about to hang up."

"I got him?"

"Who?"

"Him."

"DEAC DAMIT!! Who you got!? The clap? Drunk bastard. Who? You got two seconds and I'll…"

"I got your pimply face boyfriend."

"What? What you mean you got him?"

"Yup. call me tricky dick-man. Ha! Get it, DICK-man. HA! Like Dick Tracy and Nixon had a baby."

"Where?"

"Here. In my room. Scooped him up at the freaky leaky party this morning in horse ball sweat."

"I don't wanna know. You telling me he's in your room like right now?"

"Yes meson, dass what I said."

"Why?"

"Tole him my Tikko and Mikko will tickle his frito."

"How long he been there?"

"A minit. I think. I kinda blacked out on the sofa here in the lobby. What time is it? I'm getting party favors. Gonna boogie in Japan."

"What? Get yo ass back there and make sure he don't move. We got to secure him and get him to the court in three hours. Jeezus! I'm gonna get Chick and Jimmy. We be right down. Don't you fuckin move."

"Roger Ramjet. Over and Out. Hey Yanacita Momi Rita. You got condoms and rubber gloves on your cart?"

The fellas bound off the elevator into the lobby in serious mode. Deak is passed out again on the lobby sofa.

"Hey fool! Git up! Where is he?"

"Who?"

"Russell damnit!"

"Oh. I tole yo monkey-ass he's in my room. 107 or 8. Ask for Mikko San. I don't feel so good."

"Get up fool. Let's go."

Deak did not have the door key. "Knock Knock. Tick Tock Tikki Likki my babies. It's your samurai daddy. Open up. My hands are full of ice and yummies."

Tikko opened the door in a bathrobe looking sleepy.

"Hey baby, ask Russell to come help me bring in the stuff will ya baby-san?"

"Oh he gone go daddy-san. Say he had go now. Gave me hicky this on mi booby. Look. Cute ya? Ricky shape like booty, no? Where you be daddy-san? Go soooo long. We shower. He shower wit us. He funny little pink boy-san. Hehe."

"Where he go baby?"

"He say front desk call cab."

"Holy shit no!" Booker, Chick and Ray dashed back to the front desk.

CHAPTER 28

WHAT SAY YOU?

Earlier at 10pm - Logan County Courtroom

QUIET! QUIET! I WANT IT QUIET IN THIS COURT RIGHT NOW!

Hammering! Hammering! Hammering!

"Listen to me! Officers will clear this room and arrest anyone refusing to leave. Bailiff, get control of this room now! Throw out anyone who does not comply!"

The mob settled with McDougle's threats, though they knew he will not carry them out. The gallery settled in.

"Listen and listen well. This is a court of law and order, and not the damn rodeo. You people have been issued your last warning."

A baby cried.

"I SAID QUIET! Shut that damn baby up!!" Red McDougle finally arrived in full crimson. Forehead, ears, cheeks; all capillary red. He slammed the hammer down with crimson furry. It shattered into pieces. He froze, stared at what's left of the handle in his hand.

"Now look what you made me do! Oh hell. Let's get on with it. We all know why we're here. The members of the jury are back. Have you reached a decision?"

"Yes your honor." The Foreman rose.

"Mr. Foreman, what say you? Please read your decision to the court."

"Your honor. We the jury for the case of the State of Illiois versus Darnell Whitaker, on the two counts of murder in the first degree, we the jury find the defendant guilty on both charges."

BOOM!

A Powder keg of pandemonium exploded in the room. Cries, yells, cheers, howls, reporters scrambled, additional police officers pushed people out of the court. Officer's Butler and Sullivan stood staring at McDougle in disgust. Percy, JC, and Yuri surrounded Darnell. Barbara and Maria cannot stand, stunned, stuck in their seats.

"Officers take the prisoner back to his cell. Tomorrow is a holiday but under the circumstances I will be rendering sentencing tomorrow at 8am sharp! No holiday! NOW CLEAR THIS COURTROOM NOW!!"

"We have breaking news from Lincoln Illinois. We now go live to Desiree Justine in Lincoln with more from the Darnell Whitaker murder trial. Desiree, what's happening now?"

"Thanks Merri. In a stunning swift decision, the court ordered an emergency reconvene in the capitol murder case against Darnell Whitaker. The jury has returned with a guilty verdict on two counts of capital murder of Chuck and Elizabeth Wagner, Darnell's adopted parents here in Lincoln. There is almost uncontrollable chaos all around the courthouse now, inside and out. Tear gas, fighting, crying, yelling, protesting. This is a chaotic scene Merri!"

"Are you safe Desiree?"

"Yes, we are just across the street from the fracas which is centered on the courthouse grounds. No one thought the jury would come back so quickly but people never left the area after the case adjourned earlier tonight. They came to unanimous guilty verdict in another rapid and seemingly record breaking time for a case of this magnitude. The jury of nine men and nine women, all white, seemed to have no trouble deciding the fate of this 17-year old black Chicago teen who found himself caught up in a whirlwind, and possibly none of it of his doing. This is an unprecedented rush to justice in the state. As you know, the defense claims that there is a mysterious suspect out there who is the actual killer. No one knows for sure who and where he is and no one has come forward. The defense has people out searching but nothing has materialized. However a name and photo has recently surfaced since the court broke for jury deliberation at about six PM. The name Russell Smerkars has come up. A local notorious criminal who lives in the area. Sources say he has disappeared as of late as he was recently arraigned in this same court recently for assaulting the manager of the local Kroger store after he was caught stealing some rib eye steaks. It just so happened that that same Kroger manager mysteriously died in a suspicious house fire.

"Oh my, that is suspicious. No sign of him?"

"No and authorities want him for questioning about the deaths of Mr. Frys and his pregnant wife in that fire. And get this. Two other people who were at that Kroger the day of the assault on Mr. Frys are either missing or died recently in the daycare fire a few weeks ago you may remember. Lots of speculation but no suspect."

"Desiree, this begs the obvious question, were the Whitakers also at the Kroger when the stakes were stolen?"

"This question never came up during the trial so we don't know. Police are asking if anyone has seen him to not approach him as he may be armed and extremely dangerous. And to

contact the Lincoln police immediately by dialing 911. Happy New Year Merri."

"Uh, same to you Desiree. Any plans for tonight in Lincoln?"

"Looks like it's going to a long non-traditional New Year's eve for me and my photographer Donovan James tonight."

"Be safe out there."

"You bet. Reporting live from the Logan County Courthouse, Desiree Justine, for WGN News."

Part 6

NO HOPE NOPE

CHAPTER 29

CORNERED

Front desk said he left about 30 minutes ago." Booker pounded the desk.

"Damnit Deak, why didn't you call us sooner! Why you let him out of your sight?"

"Well I…"

"Neva'mind. Did the front desk say where he went?"

"No, he said he just called the cab company for him cuz he was drunk."

"Damn, we can't lose him. It's six o'clock, sentencing at eight. Shit!"

"Call Curtis 13."

"Who?"

"My guy 13, the cabby bro. Here's his card. He dropped us all here. He got the big ones."

"What? Shut up fool!" Jimmy scoffed.

Cabby Curtis Abernathy arrived at the hotel in 15 minutes. He said he did not come back here for anyone.

"Can you call your dispatch place and see where'd they take him?" Deak stumbled forward.

"Awe man that shit is confidential. They wont' give me that info."

Mikko and Tikko came to the lobby dressed and packed to go.

"We go now baby-san."

"Where you going my sushi sans? We had plans ya no. Mount Fuji need to erupt"

"We go now. Must work food store early. Big sale on powder for babies and face cream for men."

"Yo, my man 13. Can you take my babies to work?"

"Fosho. They some fine ass alley cats. Peeped them earlier. I got'em."

"Look elephant boy, tell you what. They mine, but for the right price or information, they can water your hose. Dig?"

"Um. Damn. Hol'up. Dispatch this 13."

"Dispatch, go'hed 13."

"Yea can you give me a 20 on that last pick up at Motel 7. He left his wallet at the hotel and I can bring it to him real quick."

"10-4 13. Pax was 10-8 Lincoln Lakes."

"Copy that. 13 will be 10-8 Lakes for drop off. Have him hold at location please."

"10-4 13. Will relay."

"Maaaan, you the dude again today. 2+2+2 equal 13. My nigga." Deacon dapped him up.

Chick, Jimmy and Booker bolted out of the lobby like a blast from a pump-action shotgun to the Dragon parked around back of the motel.

With the top down for maximum clarity, visually and mentally, Ray cranked the heater up full blast as they roared to the lakes in the cold winter early morning air. Pulling into the Lakes proper, Jimmy flipped a switch Reese installed with the re-mod that diverts the exhaust through a second set of fat pillow quiet mufflers instead of the skinny Thrush Glass-Pak screamers.

The Dragon idled quietly along the dirt road of the Lakes estate home community tucked into wooded lots. Lights out, they eyeballed the dark thick tree'd area by the light of a full moon and cloudless early morning black sky. Any movement would flash like a silver fish on a hook. The cold air keened their senesces with razor sharp awareness. They swiveled their heads side to side in search. No movement should be out here during this pre-dawn winter darkness. The Dragon purred along the dirt road as they peered through the thicket and across the moon reflecting black lakes.

"If he's here, he would have to break in someones house or head to the public cabanas with restrooms. He could run the hand dryers for heat inside the small restroom and make it toasty."

"You see that? Across the lake? Wait. Watch over there, near that little hut."

They spotted movement in the moonlit tree cover. Carefull navigation of the Dragon along the lake's edge brought them close to the cabanas. Shutting the car down, they moved on foot. Walking lightly, they heard the crack of branches and leaf crunch. They split into a triangle search approach toward the sound within the trees. Chick went into the thick a bit. Booker and Jimmy pushed towards a clearing. They stopped and listened. Russell emerged from the tree line into the clearing to cross towards the huts.

"Stop Russell. You're done. Hold it right there. Booker and Jimmy emerged from different angles.

"No. You're done ass holes." Russell leveled AJs silver .45 long barrel at them, moving the barrel from one to the next.

"First one moves get it." They froze.

"I think that will be you fat boy." Aiming at Booker. "Say good night niggaz."

Russell squeezed the trigger. In a flash, Chick blind sided him with a ferocious Dick Butkus rib cracking tackle. The pistol fired up in the air and out of Russell's hand. Jimmy jumped on top of Russell and started pounding him. Booker grabbed the gun.

"Thats enough! Get up jerk wod." Jimmy wrestled him up.

Nose, mouth and eyes bleeding, Jimmy put him in a full nelson hold like a vice grip and walked him to the Dragon.

They reached the edge of the clearing near the car. Time to get him to court.

"That's far enough. Let him go and drop the gun. NOW!"

CHAPTER 30

SHOTS OF LOVE

Enzo and Manni emerged from the thicket, both pointing silver plated Colt .45's long barrels at the group.

"I said drop the gun and drop the kid."

"Awe geez thanks guys. I knew the Outfit would come through. You guys are the real deal." Russell struggled to his feet.

"Who the fuck are you guys?" Booked asked.

"Don't matta who we is. We'll take him from here. Thanks for doing our work coons." Enzo scoffed as Manni frisked them for weapons, removing Booker's snug nose .45 from his belt.

"You not the grease that had been tailing Darnell." Jimmy dropped his hands.

"Yea them ass holes don't tail nothing no more. Services no longer required, capisi? Get yer fuckin hands up spook."

"What you want with Russell?" Booker tried to inch his foot toward the gun on the ground.

"Don't get fuckin slick out here. Just freeze like we told'ja. We got our orders. None of your concern."

"So you think we gonna just turn over like whores?" Booker also dropped his hands.

"From our position, odds are in our favor. You go ass up bitches. You flunk math or sumptin? Two guns versus no guns equal one head shot each."

"Orders from who? The Outfit? The fuck you doing down here anyways?" Chick pushed to prolong the issue.

"We don't ask how high or why. Job security, capisci?. Now enough of this monkey-ass shit. Turn around. All four yooz. Do it NOW!"

"Hey what's this? I'm with you guys, right? You came to get me the fuck outta here right? No hard feelings with AJ. Right?" Russell pleaded.

"Shut up fuck face. You stink like and un-flushed turd. You the reason we down in this dirt hole in the first place. Making all kinds of noise. Fuckin up the program. You a waste of a fuckin jerk off. Now quit yer flappin and say yer prayers. Best if you look up to the sky for your last view. Make peace with the moon and the stars on your way out. Stand closer together, two by two. One in front of the other. One bullet will go straight through to the next head. Heel to toe. Move it in! Tighter, tighter. Hold still." Enzo pushed.

"Yea, like jumpball in that basketball shit you monkeys play. We the fuckin refs and you jungle monkeys just got ejected. So the question is before I blow this whistle, do you want it in the face or the back of the head, cuz we can come around front ya no. Don't mean two shits to us." Manni growled.

"Tell you idiots what. Move in closer to the tree line. Don't want the kiddies to stumble on you till the spring after the animals and bugs pick you clean. Move!" Enzo pushed them on.

"Hey Enzo, after they go down, I think we pull their pants down like they gay bangers in the woods. With the white boy on top in the superior position. Whatdaya say, huh? These fuckin moolies."

"I like that. Yea, it'll look like a goody two-shoer farmer caught them in the act and wanted to rid the planet of you fags bangin in the woods. I'll get the Polaroid from the car to send proof back to the Don. Trophy shots. He loves those. He, he." Enzo gaffed.

"Look fellas. How about you take the kid and we get the fuck outta here. We want him gone too. He is just a side job. We ain't got no beef with you guys," Booker tried to reason.

"We have orders too ya no. This a win win where we go back to our bosses with good reports. Chicken-head here is dead and so are his black gang bangers." Enzo moved the silver Colt back and forth at their faces.

"Look guys, if we don't come back and they see this was a mob hit, streets will be red real soon. We can avoid all that. No need for this twerp to put that on you two. Bodies will fall around the city, I guarantee you. The gangs will unite and rise up against the Outfit. You guys are out numbered in the city when we come together. You don't want the Don putting that on your heads" Jimmy turned with a plea.

"Side job my ass. We saw you looking all over for him in your pussy purple hot rod. You did our work for us. We just followed you following him. That fuckin car you got can be seen for miles. Couldn't miss it on the streets. Stood out like a boner in massage parlor. We just let yoooz drive around for us. Thanks. Whoever said you shines are lazy? Sheeeiiit. I may have to get me one of them black whores when I get back to the city to do some work for me. How about your bitch pretty nigger?" Manni shoved the gun in Chicks side.

"You won't be needing that gold chain any longer. I'll take that. Think your stink'n whore wife will let me bang her with your chain wrapped around my dick? Ha! Turn the around and shut up! Enough of this shit. Put your hands in your pockets. Start walking. Times up!" Enzo pushed them along to the edge of the clearing.

"A little further closer to the trees. Now on your knees. Do it!! I'm gonna love that car you leaving me. Thanks. Be my little gift to the Don." Enzo chuckled.

"Ok, say good-night Dick. Remember, we can shoot faster than you can run. Three, two,…

Several swooshes were heard, followed by both gangsters grunting. Then POW! POW! The crew and Russell flinched.

"What the fuck!" Chick whispered.

They turned around and saw Enzo and Manni hanging upside down by their feet ten feet off the ground.

"What the hell?" Seeing the situation, Russell took a step for one of the dropped guns. SWOOSH!

In an instant he was also swooped up by his feet in another rope snare ten feet up, hanging from a thick oak branch like the others. Dangling like snared rabbits, they twirled and spun with arms flailing, cursing.

Chick was about to run.

"STOP! Don't move! You'll be next." Jimmy froze in place hands outstretched.

"Wait. Listen," Booker perked up his ears.

Then a swathoop, swathoop, swathoop!

"OUCH!" All three hanging rabbits cried out.

The dangling trio tried to reach for their lower legs to feel what just stung them in their calfs. But they could not reach their lower legs while hanging upside down.

"Shhhhhh." Booker put a finger to his lips. Forest silence.

The sun began to peek over the horizon through the trees.

"Meezeh?" They heard through the silence.

"Eh khad she kh-oht-hem." Booker answered turning his head left.

"Lih-khah-sote-eem dham" The response came from the woods on the right.

Emerging from the thicket, eight camouflaged members of the African Israelites' Sayeret Matkal emerged along with Darryl Reese.

"Reese! How the fuck? Damn man!" Booker approached him in relief.

"A thank you would do these dudes a solid." Darryl looked up at three hanging bodies.

"Oh shit. Thank you my brothers. Thank you all." Jimmy approached him also.

"Ready. Aim. Fire!" One of the camouflaged manhunters called out.

Three more darts stick into the goons and Russell's calfs of their limp but conscious hanging bodies. Arms no longer flailing. Drool began spider-webbing from their mouths.

"Did you kill them?" Booker looked at the bodies closer.

"No, just put to sleep with shots of sodium pentothal. We will be interrogating them. Thy won't remember a thing when we are done with them."

"Then what?" Chick asked watching the process unfold.

"Then they will end up back on the streets of Chicago." One of the soldiers responded whlie quickly wrapping up the bodies.

"Oh shit. Thy'll be cak in the city with no trophy and no real explaination to Donny boy. They fucked bro." Jimmy looked on at the specatacle.

The two goons were lowered, hands and feet zip tied. Black hoods synched around their necks. Within 60 seconds they were bagged, tagged, and taken away through the woods.

"What about the kid?" Booker called out to them.

Pzzzziiit! A direct shot from a small caliber round cut the rope and Russell's body hit the ground.

"Take him. He's yours. You need him, right?" The Sayeret Matkal team disappeared through the tree maze as emerging daylight made silhouettes of the bagged body and soldier parade that scurried through the woods.

The trunk of the Dragon slammed closed. The exhaust switch flipped to Glass Pack. Dirt and gravel roared a dusty rooster tail out of Lincoln Lakes.

Sunrise 7:07 am.

CHAPTER 31

BIRTHDAY SENTENCE

All rise! This Special New Year's Day sentencing hearing will commence. The Honorable Judge Howard McDougle presiding." The court bailiff's barritone boomed over the crown noise inside the courtroom.

"Be seated. Counselors, good to see all of you here early and on-time this morning. Thank you all for coming on this brand New Year's day. I know this day is supposed to be a holiday for us all. But for the Wagners, well, there will be no more holidays. On a bright note, today is the first day of the rest of our lives. And today is also year 18 for our defendant. I would say happy birthday to you Mr. Whitaker but that does not seem appropriate at this time. This should be an exciting day and time in ones' young life, but here we are. Well, we all understand the urgency of this matter and the need to facilitate swift justice for such a horrible crime. Therefore we will proceed without any further delays and anymore unruly outbursts. The seriousness of this crime cannot not be understated. Loss of life like this is never an easy thing for any of us. But this crime in particular has taken away some of the most sacred DNA of this country. It tore the heart out of this historic American community. It brought an abrupt and unwanted end to the Lincoln name. Counselor, is your client of sound mind and body?"

"Your honor we object to this proceeding and consider this a rush to justice. We ask for a mis-trial…"

"Denied."

"Then a postponement be granted until more evidence can come to light."

"Objection your honor. Defense counsel has had ample time to gather evidence. If you are referring to the fictional charter the defendant has concocted, then we will be waiting forever in the limitless time of outer space in his fantasy universe, your honor."

"Your honor, for the sake of decency for the people of the court and this community, this is a Federal and State holiday as well as the young man's birthday. Can you see to it to grant the people their earned holiday time of rest and re-energizing? Don't you think he has been through enough already? I mean what is the hurry anyway?" JC Monroe stood and delivered from behind the defense desk.

"Ms. Monroe, I completely understand your concerns but this is a highly unusual case. The state judiciary board approved of this sentencing hearing under these circumstances in an emergency session last night. And all aspects were discussed. I am following the rule of the sanctioning body of the this court and the state which has federal oversight attached to it. So all parties have weighed in on this. The gravity of the circumstances warrant this immediate action towards swift justice. I apologize to the court for any hardships this may have caused. Those on duty will recieve holiday bonus pay. Therefore we need to get on with it so we can salvage what will be left of the day. Unless of course you decide to continue prolonging these proceedings. We will proceed."

"But your honor there is great speculation that your personal feelings towards the murder of your cousin is a driving bias. Therefore we request that you recuse yourself from this proceedings immediately before making this ruling from a biased and tainted lens." JC countered from in front of the defense desk now.

Gallery murmurs buzzed.

Hammerieng.

"Ladies and gentlemen of the court. I do have a new hammer, one made of steel, and no, not vibranium, (chuckles form the right). Please help me refrain from using it today. As you can see, I did allow one TV camera and one newspaper camera to come in today. For exactly this reason you see here. Now their little show will be televised. Once again defense counsel is attempting to make a three ring circus out of this serious matter. As stated earlier, and I will waste the people's time again by repeating it, there will be no recusal based on the recommendations of the board. You can take it up in appeal counselor."

"But your honor…"

"Sit down Ms. Monroe! The matter is closed. On to the business at hand. We have two counts of murder in the first degree filed by the state. Is this the charge you are remaining counselor?"

"Yes your honor. Murder One, two counts remain in order."

"Very well. Defense counselors? What say you to these charges and what are your preferences?"

"Your honor, defense recommends a lesser charge of Man 2 due to the emotional aspect of this crime. If my client were actually guilty of this crime, it is obviously a crime of passion by a teenager and not a crime of calculated intent which man-one requires. The prosecution did not prove this intent."

"Counselor, let me remind you that we are not here to re-litigate the trial. Your recommendations please."

"We recommend Man 2, ten years, parole after three, given the lack of criminal history."

"Very well. I understand your recommendations, thank you. I have taken both into consideration. Given the gravity and heinousness of this violent act and the utter callousness of the defendant to willingly take the life of his adopted parents who spent no less than five years researching and waiting to adopt him, it appears that his level of hate and calculating coldness along with a heightened level of suppressed rage, clearly demonstrated since his arrival here in Lincoln, this peaceful town, that frankly, the worse crimes that recently happened here of late, are a far cry from cow theft or veterinarian poisoning.

That the defendant poses a serious and dangerous threat to this community and society at large. The ability to craft such an evil plot speaks volumes to his depth of hate and accepted level of horror. Frankly, since he arrived here, the horrible deaths that have happened, which seemed accidental, are now under investigation as criminal acts. Are these all coincidental? We will soon find out. I would hate to find a link between those deaths and the Wagner's murders at the hands of the defendant. How wrong we all were, even myself, who worked on your case for as many years to bring you here.

You not only let me down, but the literally hundreds of people across the nation who had the name Darnell Whitaker on their desks as a case model and ideal candidate for the ideal child for interracial adoption. So my ruling is not about me Ms. Monroe and company. It's not about your team of my most average law students back in the day. I am as far removed from this as I can possibly be, except for the sorrow I naturally feel for the loss of my cousin of course.

Matter of fact, if this happened to her in another way, yes I would recused myself automatically. But this is about the American people and the democratic form of justice and policy creation that we practice to find and preserve truth. Not by the influence of extreme minorities, but by the greater body of the people who are affected by any ruling. Be it votes by a majority jury or votes by a majority public. I defend the constitutional rights of all Americans and all citizens of the great state of Illinois. And it is my duty to protect them."

One person started to clap then backed off. Multiple eyeballs snapped in the direction of the clapper. Maria rolled her eyes at the clapper mouthing, "m-o-r-o-n."

"Does the defendant have anything to say?"

"No your honor." Percy reponded.

"Very well. Then will the defendant please rise. In the capitol murder case of the State of Illinois versus Darnell Whitaker, and to show that I do have concern for this broken family, you will be remanded to Joliet State prison so as your father will be able to visit you, if he so chooses. Your sentencing there will be as follows:

Given the fact that you are considered an adult as of today, for the count of Murder One of Charles Wagner, twenty-five years to life. And for the charge of Murder One of Mrs. Elizabeth Wagner, twenty-five years to life. Both terms will be carried out consecutively. At the end of the second term, if you are still alive, you will be put to death by lethal injection."

The courtroom exploded!

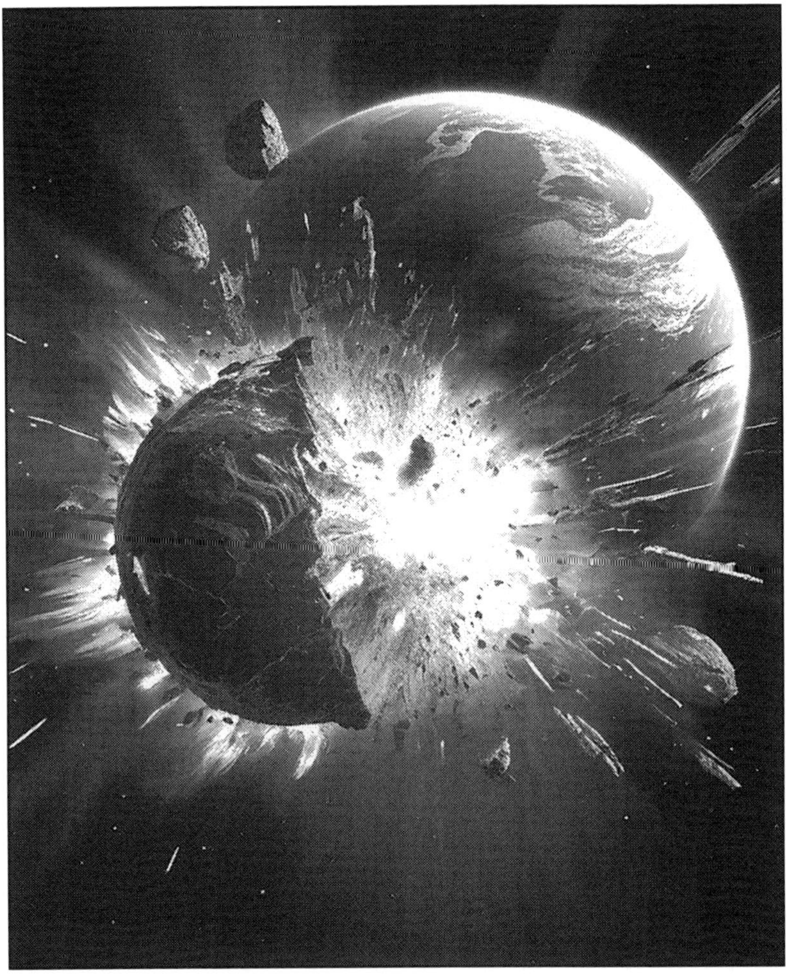

CHAPTER 32

BOOM BABY!

Hammering!!

"Bailiff, get the prisoner out here now!! ORDER. ORDER I SAY! ORDER IN THIS COURT!!!

Everyone in the room was up and yelling. Threatening gestures pointed at each side. Some on the right stood in their chairs pumping their fists in victory yelling USA! USA! USA! Officers Bruce Butler and Ryan Sullivan ran to cover Darnell. Percy, Yuri and JC looked around at the bedlam like bombing drones were coming in from all directions. Maria and Barbara let out a cry and held each other. Five of Frongello's supporters wearing black leather vests with the words, Corn Fed and Red, stitched on their backs, surrounded Frongello. Their cocoon poised to swing on anyone looking for a piece of Frongello.

McDougle standing, hammered his Thor hammer to no avail.

"ORDER! ORDER! ORDER!"

Like a mid-evil field of battle, both sides of the mob faced each other poised to a demolition derby collision across the isle divide.

"Officers, get the prisoner out of here NOW!"

Darnell looked at Percy in horror. The officers froze in conflict. Darnell grabbed Percy. They clinched each others arms.

"I said now! Get him out of here or you both will do hard time after I fire you asses. Now GO!!"

BANG!

A woman screamed like she was shot in the ass.

The twin fifteen-foot wood and brass doors of the court slammed open. All of the mealy stopped. Mouths' dropped at the sight. Like the Hebrew slave once Pharaoh, Russell was dragged into court bound and bloodied like Moses brought to Ramses. Booker, Jimmy and Chick dragged him by his shoulders. The ear-splitting extreme decibels fell to zero.

"What the hell is this!" McDougle jumped from his judges seat. "Get out of my court! Officers, stop these men NOW!" McDougle pointed his Oden Hammer at them as if lightening was suppose to spit out. Percy stepped forward looking at Booker, nodding affirmative. Percy turned his head slowly around his shoulders with angry victorious eyes zoomed in towards McDougle.

"Your honor, I present to the court the real killer of Elizabeth and Chuck Wagner. Russell Smerkars."

Booker and Jimmy dropped Russell's limp body to the floor. Donovan James panned and zoomed his camera in. Desiree pointed her wireless shotgun mic at the action, smiling a devilish grin.

"The hell you say?" McDougle leaned forward with an angry yet worried look on his face.

"That's him! Thats him! He killed my mother and father. That's him!" Darnell tore loose from the officers running over to Russell.

"What in God's name are you talking about boy! Is this some kind of circus stunt counselor? Get these people out of here!"

"No your honor. We have been trying to convince the court that my client is not the killer. But this court did not listen. Well, we have the killer in court now." Percy moved to the center of the courtroom between his son and Russell and McDougle.

"Your honor. The defense is living in a fantasy. This is part of their little ghetto theater. This is not the killer. They have no proof. Just someone they found and beat to a pulp to make him say anything they want him to say. Hell I would confess if they beat me like that. Look at that poor kid for God's sake! Who beats a child like that? Monsters your honor! Monsters!" An animated Frongello broke free from his ring of leathered Red Boy goons.

"Mr. Whitaker. I am warning you. You and your whole team will be stuffed in one cell for six months for this crap. You have no proof. Get him and your thugs out of here, now!"

"He is the proof!" Percy bellowed larger than life, filling the stunned room. Heads snapped in his direction as he faced McDougle down from the center isle. He stood taller, his shoulders larger, broader. His chest stretched the lapels of his suit jacket. His fists balled in defiance. His creased scowl menacingly assured.

"Young man. Did you kill the Wagners?" McDougle came down from his bench leaning down to Russell's face, hoping to connect with his underhanded nuance. Russell peered up at McDougle trying to speak but the drugs were too powerful.

"Ya see, nothing. Everyone clear this courtroom and get this prisoner to the penitentiary, IMMEDIATELY DAMNIT!" The crimson McDougle yelled even louder than Percy.

Booker shook Russell. He could not muster a response. Chick slapped him in the face. A woman screamed and fainted in the back of the court, nothing from Russell.

McDougle face to face with Percy now, "Counsel, you have really out-done yourself this time. I thought I taught you better than this. Now I see I failed the three of you. You are no better than your psycho son. Get out of my sight. You all disgust me."

"Your honor, he did confess!" Booker stepped to the judge.

"To who? To you? Ha! Look at him. He can barely speak. What, you gangster slapped him into confession? Who and what do you think I am? Some sort of Gomer Pyle? We'll gaawwwllie sarge. I guess he done did do it! Officers get these gang bangers out of my court now!"

The stunned silence was broken by the sound of funky music that boomed from the back of the gallery,

"I gotcha, uh huh huh!
Thought I didn't see ya now didn't ya?
Uh huh huh!
You tried to sneak by me now didn't ya?
Uh huh huh!
Now give what you promised, give it here!
C'mon!

The Texas funk of Joe Tex snapped heads to the back of the courtroom. Emerging from the back, Stanley Greenwood Jr. and Keith Allen carried a boom box forward to the front of the court.

"You want proof? We got proof." Stanley and Keith walked to the front and turned to the gallery of the stunned on-lookers frozen stare.

"And who in God's name are you?" McDougle appearing more confident with a sarcastic smirk.

"Well thank you sir for recognizing that I do come in God's name. I am Stanley."

"And I'm Keef. Sup?"

"Well wa da do da! It's the Splib-Tations. What now counselor? Your bag of tricks just keeps getting you more time in the clink I hope you know. On with the show! Jeezus Mary and Jack-Asses." McDougle's neck swelled thicker, redder.

"My dad is Pastor of Bridge of Life Community Church in Atlanta."

"Oh that place, a heathen's den. What do you want son? Are you part of the circus also? My God counselor, you have the church spun into your theatrics? Now you want to take a dump in the house of God? Don't you ever quit?" McDougle laughing now.

Percy looked at Yuri, JC, then over to Barbara. Not sure what was happening.

"Sir, I have proof. Proof he did that murder sir." Stanley pointed to the ceiling.

"What proof son?"

"On tape. I'll play it."

"Wai, wai, wait! Do not play that tape! It must be introduced as evidence. This case is closed." Frongello quickly stepped towards McDougle with a worried look on his face.

"You said you want proof sir. Here it is. Don't you all here want proof who really killed the Wagners?" Percy looked upon the entire gallery for a response. The pro-Darnell side hollered various forms of yes!

"Your honor, in light of these unusual circumstances this tape must be heard. According to…"

"Yea yea yea Mr. Yendel. You don't have to cite case law to me. Jeezus!"

Stanley turned to the stunned and puzzled gallery mob.

"Y'all want me to play it?" Many nodded yes on both sides. Others looked worried. Someone shouted, "PLAY THE TAPE!" More people joined in, "PLAY THE TAPE! PLAY THE TAPE!"

"Your honor, if this evidence can prove innocence of my client, you must allow it. You taught us that. And the cameras don't lie your honor," Percy turned to Donovan's video camera recording the entire event. Desiree Justine swiveled her shotgun microphone from Percy to McDougle. All eyes on McDougle now.

"Your honor?"

More hesitation, sweat, a crimson tide flooded his blood soaked bird's nest of frazzled red hair. He was on fire.

"Fine. Play the damn tape. But I'm warning you. This is it. Jail time for you all. I promise you!"

Keith handed Stanley a cassette tape to insert. He turned up the volume then pressed play:

"I hate cops.
They suck ass.
They get in my way
when I'm being jazz
Stole me a car
they want it back
I crashed that fucker
I ain't given jack
They think they smarter than me
I can run and hide
I'm too slick for them
cuz I gotta get mine."

"Yea! Cool man. Keep going!"

"I ain't scared of them or the mob
I get rid of people that blow my job
Burn down daycares or blow up a house
Hell I ain't no little scared mouse
They see me when I'm cookin
I get rid of them then I'm bookin.
I shoot him pop pop in his face
You won't find me any day
You squeal on me I shoot you in the face
Moms and pops in the alley no chase

*I bury chicks under the road
and burn Tropics to the ground
That's how I get down
You see me steal steaks
I make you pay
I'm the man cuz I goth them all today
They think I'm dumb
I cap them for fun
You cross me then you done
Redrum Redrum Redrum
It's the color that I done
Now I do it for fun
If you see me you better run
See me in the mirror
Redrum Redrum Redrum."*

"What you think? You like it?"

"Uh, um, man! That's some dope cool stuff. You see. You can do songs. Man you should make a record on that. It would sell!"

"Maaaan, you think so? That felt good. I'll call it Redrum. You got any more weed?"

"Uh, yea. Knock it out man. Them some powerful lyrics."

"What's lyrics?'

"Ya no, the words. They felt so real."

"They are real. I live that shit cuz I'm a mobster."

"What you mean?"

"Don't say nothin, but they brought me in."

"Who?"

"The mob. They hear ya no? Watchin that nigger boy. But they tried to off me so I capped one of them in the face and took his car. They lookin for me now."

"Why?"

"That's what I'm sayin! Why they wanna off me? I did what they asked me to do! I took out all the witnesses who saw me at

Kroger! I proved myself like they asked me! Torched the house and Daycare and buried that bitch at that stupid Tropics bar. Fuck, we even burned it down! Ha! They know I am the real deal. Now they wanna cap me! ME! Well I showed them who's the real mobster. Took one of them out, now they looking for me. That's why I gotta keep movin. Man I need some money."

"Ummm, well I ain't got that. But maybe you can win at the card tables inside. Wanna try? You can get some credit. I'll cover for you but only for ten."

"Naw. I need to get outta here."

Silence in the court.

CHAPTER 33

DUH

Oden-Son Thor Fury Hammering!

Jubilee roared in the courtroom. One side looked confused and bewildered, stuck in their chairs, the other side hugged, cried, hi-fived, fist pumped, and thanked God like the rapture just scooped them up. Donovan walked his camera up to the front of the court to cover the cheering, then whip-panned the camera to McDougle.

A stunned McDougle looked at the scene. Cognizant of the camera, he pulled back his hammer. He sat in contemplate and humiliation amongst the joy. He stood raising both hands above his head signaling for, pleading for silence.

"Please, please. All of you please. This is obviously some explosive evidence. However the court must know if this is actually the perpetrator. We don't know if this is him. We must be sure. And right now he is in no condition to respond to questioning. Therefore I cannot allow this crazy testimony to influence my decision to…"

"He he he he he heeeeeeeee." Russell still on his knees, he creeked a sinister sound.

"Mr. Smerkers? Mr. Smerkers. Are you Russell Smerkers?"

"He he heeeeeeeeeee. You don't know me."

"Mr. Smerkers can you hear me?" McDougle pushed.

"He he heeeeeee. Now you love me, don't you? You love me now. You love Russell now. He he heeeeee."

"Mr. Smerkers was that you on that tape with the music? Did you hear that? Did you say those words? Are they true Russell Smerkers?"

"He he heeeeeeee. Now you know me. I sing. I dance. I shoot. I kill. I burn you. I bury you. I am for real. You fuck with me I do my job. Cuz I am the mob. Now I am the mob. I cannot be stopped. Those fuckin people. And that nigger boy. Should have shot him too. He fucked my leg up. Got lucky. I'll kill him next. Where is he? NIGGER!!!!! Now you all will know my name, I am the mob, I am Russell Smerkers, the great!"

The stunned court crowd moaned.

"Bailiff. Take him out of my court." McDougle directed with his Thor Hammer.

Cheers erupted again. People on the right stormed out of the courtroom heated and dejected. Those on the left celebrated.

"Your honor. This confession proves my client's, my son's, innocence. My son." Percy stepped to the judge.

McDougle walked away from Percy and back to his thick padded throne on the grand judge bench platform and dropped down into it, bewildered.

"Case dismissed. Everybody get the hell out of my court!"

Red hair disheveled, face not crimson, now ivory. McDougle closed his eyes to not look upon his defeat.

"We have some incredible breaking news from Lincoln in the Darnell Whitaker double murder case. Desiree Justine is in Lincoln. Desiree what bizarre turn of events have just unfolded."

"For absolute certain, this is an amazing turn of events here in Lincoln where people are up in arms in confusion and

heightened emotions. Just moments after the jury found Darnell Whitaker guilty of double murder of his parents, the 18- year old adopted black son of Chuck and Liz Wagner, a white couple from here in Lincoln, and the last remaining decedents of former President Abraham Lincoln, Judge Howard McDougle sentenced him to a surprising long term sentence followed by the death sentence.. However at an eleventh hour seemingly desperate and unorthodox play by the defense team, a bound and beaten Russell Smerkers was dragged into the courtroom by some unknown associates of councilman Whitaker. I've never seen anything like this. Judge McDougle threatened to jail the entire defense team with what appeared to be a stunt by the defense but a seemingly incoherent Smerkers could only babble a few words. In a highly intense moment for all, a young waiter from the Blue Dog Inn here in Lincoln played a tape with Smerkers confessing his guilt. And get this, not only did he confess to the Wagner murders, but also the murders of Jay Frys and his pregnant wife in a deliberate house fire, the fiery deaths of Michael Mansfields and nine other people, including several babies in the horrible daycare center fire here in Lincoln. And he confessed to killing Mrs. Ruthy Martins as well as burning down the famous Tropics Restaurant here in Lincoln. Just an incredible turn of events. A groggy Smerkers proudly admitted he was the person confessing these murders on a cassette tape played in court. Unbelievable! As you have seen over the past weeks of this trial, the town is split almost down the middle of guilt or innocence for Darnell Whitaker. This incredible confession blows the lid off of this entire awful, awful situation here in Lincoln."

"Desiree, What happens to Darnell now?"

"Well, Darnell is a free man. And he is now a legal man, as his 18th birthday is today, New Year's day."

'Oh my, what a bittersweet birthday present."

"Yes, the candles of freedom shine bright for Darnell Whitaker who can celebrate his exoneration and freedom in the face of losing his adopted parents in an awful and tragic way."

"What of his life now? Isn't his biological father also his attorney?"

You are correct in asking what now. Only time will answer this question. Reporting live from the incredible finally to a truly sad, sad situation for so many, I'm Desiree Justine from Lincoln for WGN."

Great work Desiree. In other legal news, a suit has been filed against the owners of Garrett Popcorn, by Duane Brooks of Arlington, claiming he invented the famous Chicago Mix popcorn while serving prison time at Jolliet State prison ten years ago.

CHAPTER 34

PACK OUT

Any more boxes to come down to the car? My back is screamin like a howler monkey."

"Naw, that's the last one Officer Bruce. Thanks."

"How many times I gottta tell you. It's Bruce. Just Bruce. Got it? You earned it. Never met anyone quite like you kiddo."

"Never will. Thanks." Darnell cracked a difficult smile.

"Been a pleasure serving you D-Dawg!" They dapped each other up with a complicated dap they worked out in the jail lock-up.

"Hey meathead. You forgot something!" Maria called out from the upstairs window of the Wagner house.

"Better go get that. You definitely don't want to leave that BEE-HIND. May need to hit it and quit it," Butler smiled while he stuffed boxes in the trunk of the GTO.

Darnell looked at him not sure what he meant.

"Be right there doofus!" He called up to Maria.

Percy, JC, Yuri, the S.S. crew, and Barbara watched him trot back into the house. He gated quickly through the yard full of people who cared about him. All celebrating his victory while still mourning the loss of Liz and Chuck.

"Do you think he is permanently affected by all of this Percy?" JC asked.

"If he is, he's masking it well." Percy watched him go inside the house.

"That was too close." Yuri said watching Darnell go.

"To damn close." JC responded.

"Why didn't you play the hotel recording from Desiree?" Yuri asked.

"I was about to but something told me to hold that trump card for another day." Percy gazed off in thought while speaking.

"But that could have been the break we needed to keep up the search." Yuri side-eyed Percy.

"Listen Yuri. Faith is a strong thing. If you have it, use it. If not, lose it."

"I don't understand you sometimes Percy. You be taking chances that are not really necessary. Skirting the law, twisting it. We weren't trained like that." Yuri rubbing his jaw.

"We? Where I'm from Yuri, the law is what you make it. Hey, we learned from the best right? If you ain't cheating you ain't tryin."

"Does that mean we are dirty sons of bitches also?" Yuri froze.

"I ain't claiming that shit my nigga," JC smacked Yuri on his ass.

"Hey!"

"Ohhhh. Niiiiiiggaaa, My Nigga. I see now" Yuri smiled and finally got it.

"Yo, what did I forget up here. Don't we have it all at the car?" Darnell looked around the room.

"Two things, small but important. This." Maria held up his journal.

"Oh dang, thanks." He hopped over to take it from her.

"And this." She lunged into him wrapping her arms around his neck smashing her lips into his. He locked up like a prison door. Her squeezing unlocked the bars. He reached around her and pulled her in apprehensively tight. The powerful kiss erupted into a deep long adventurous journey. All of the sharing, caring, laughing, crying, arguing, playing, discovering, debating, crying, and worrying wrapped up in one lip lock. Feeling every moment of togetherness since the day he first set foot on Lincoln soil. She bit his bottom lip not wanting to release it. She buried her head in his neck. She started to cry.

"Darnell with two Ls," she cry-chuckled and sniffed up her tears. "I thought you were this snob dweebo. Then you became my hero. My friend. My Yang to your Yin. You are all kinds of stuff to me and I will always love you, this, us, here, now… all of it."

He swallowed hard. Could not speak. He pulled away a bit nose to nose. They looked within each other.

"I'm not asking for anything Darnell. I'm sharing my heart with you. This is God. One day you will figure out how to do the same. That's all."

"I, I."

"Yea. Me too. My Avenger. Go fly. Go fight. Go win. Just come back. Okay?"

"Okay." He pulled her in tighter, feeling each other's heartbeats.

"Oh God."

HONK! HONK!

"Your universe awaits. Better not keep it waiting. It's ugly out there in the cosmic.

"Maria, I, we…"

"Shhhhhh. Go get'em. You will know what to do when the time is right. You know where I'll be. Right here in ole Abe's bumb-fuck ghetto."

"But how do I do this without you?"

"Well."

"Well what?"

"You do it well. Now go before I do something."

"What do you mean?"

She peered a sulty gaze into him, exhaling in his mouth. They kissed again. This time deeper. Now they felt the heat. Their embrace stronger, tighter. Kissing for hunger now. Kissing like deep diving into the ocean searching for an opening. Needing each others lips to breath.

"Oh damn." He said in release.

"Yep. That's it. The buzz feed baby. Now you really need to go before I DO SOMETHING ELSE!"

"Yea. Yes. Ok. Wow."

"So hot now."

"C'mon. Let's go soldier girl."

"Chili Solja gerl you mean."

"Hell yea. Bustin them cosmic asses on a regular. You a bad-ass Maria. My flavor."

"Chili?"

"With Funyons."

"I'm weird? Dude really? Ha! C'mon let's go Kimo."

"Kimo?"

"Kimosabe. My Chief. Makes me Pocahantus."

"Yea. Let us tomato Poca."

"Now you speaking my lingo baby! Ha ha!!

He grabbed her hand and the journal. They emerged on the porch. The gathering mass cheered them as they made a b-line between the group to the awaiting cars. They moved through the mass like a wedding march. Just needed rice to throw and the GTO to ride off into the sunset.

A piece of paper fell from the journal as they walked to the ready cars. Percy picked it up. Unfolded it. Stopped in his tracks and read it. He looked up. Looked down at the paper. His mouth opened but nothing came out. He re-folded the paper and pocketed it. Wrong time. Wrong place. Right answer. He silently mouthed, "SON-OF-A-BITCH."

"Well this is it folks. Journeys end." Percy announced to the group with a non-celebratory look on his face. Covering his questions about what he just read. His wiggle waggled wicked now. He looked at JC with a precarious gaze. She returned the stare realizing something big just wiggled out of him.

"Journey is just beginning," Barbara beamed with her arm around Darnell.

The gathering crowd gave their good-byes. They all shortly reflected on the good times they had as the horror of it all hovered over like a thunder cloud about to drop a tornado on their heads. Brian Cook dapped-up Darnell strong, insisting they will meet again in Chicago and hoop together.

No grand party send off. No long table of foods from all the farms. No Von Brown's BBQ. No drunk Sammy. No music in the trees. Only sincere half solemn moods to nibble on.

Dez brought him a package wrapped in brown paper.

"What's this?"

"I think you know. But it's two things, books and records, some of the best. I'll let you figure out the rest. An honor son. You are special and I feel like we are related. I'll leave the Alto in the corner for you."

"Thanks Dez. Keep smoking that butt."

"You know it kid."

"Everyone looked at them and each other wondering what the hell they were talking about.

"Well son. You riding with us or them?"

"You mean the Galaxy 500 or the Goat? Sorry dad. I'm all about that GOAT life."

"That's cuz you smell like a goat," Maria moved in and gave him a peck on his cheek. She backed away crossing her arms, rubbing her goose bumps. She turned and walked away sniffling, not wanting to see the final motion of departure.

With the top down, Darnell jumped in the back seat. Turned around up on his knees and saw his past turned future turned past that may be his future. He scanned every eyeball with thanks and gratitude. He held his stare at Stanley Greenwood. Stanley pounded his chest with his fist. He saw a taxi in the distance with an odd looking tall lanky dude standing next to it. The dude waved a small wave. He locked on but he did not recognize him nor return the wave.

"Hey Unk Chick. Who's that tall lanky dude over there at the cab?"

All three amigos looked back at the Deacon.

"Let's just say, divine intervention," Chick laughed his golden toothed dimpled smile. Booker looked at Jimmy in the front seat. "Sheeeeiiiiittt.!" The three burst into a hollering laugh.

"Bye everyone. Thanking you is not enough. I will just say that I will be back. Gotta go figure some things out now."

Tears and sniffles broke the silence.

"Go get 'em tiger!"

"We love you Darnell!"

"Always welcome home son!"

"Moyee Woot! My dawg!"

They all waved good-byes. Maria, back at the house, on the porch with a two finger peace sign raised high above her head, strong and proud.

"Ready to hit it?" Jimmy looked back at Darnell.

"Yup."

"Hit it and quit it baby! Be out this bitch." CHick buckled his seat belt.

"Need road tunes. Buckle up." Jimmy shoved an eight-track in the deck.

James Brown screamed. The guitar dropped a lick. The JB Horns threw in hits and James screamed again:

I'm back!
I'm Back!
I'm Back!
I'm Back!
Get up off that thang and dance till you feel better
Get up off that thang till you sing it now!
Get up off that thang and dance till you feel better
Get up off that thang try and to relief that pressure!
Get up off that thang and shake till you feel better

"Let's git it!" Jimmy stomped the gas. Four heads snapped back. The Glass Pack Thrush mufflers screamed bloody murder under the dragons mighty roar. When the smoke cleared, twin fat black fishtailing skid marks snaked their autograph on Lincoln Ave.

Maria shook that thing hard and purposeful on the porch to the rhythm of her memories. The mass huddle watched them pull away. At the other end of the block, the blacked out back-seat window of a Chrysler LaBaron rolled down. Two almond eyes peered at the celebration send off. A half-smiling Yolanda Whitaker can go back to the rehab center in Chicago in peace now.

The City of Big Shoulders has its team back. Now the work begins…

So you ask, "what about the Will?"

The saga continues in:

BOOK 5

LINCOLN'S CURSE

Coming soon…

Book 1 Songs - Lincoln's Touch

What's Going On - Marvin Gaye - 1971

Ball of Confusion - Temptations 1970

Band of Gold - Freda Payne - 1970

Pusherman - Curtis Mayfield - 1972

Psychedelic Shack - Temptations - 1970

Disco Lady - Johnnie Taylor - 1976

Don't Call Me Nigger, Whitey - 1969

Who's That Lady - Isley Brothers - 1973

Chocolate City - Parliament - 1975

I Gotcha - Joe Tex - 1972

Papa's Don't Take No Mess - James Brown - 1973

Book 2 Songs - Lincoln's Son

In The Ghetto - Rick James - 1981

Family Affair - Sly and the Family Stone - 1971

Smiling Faces Sometimes - The Undisputed Truth - 1971

Clouds - Chaka Khan - 1980

A Horse With No Name - America - 1972

25 or 6 to 4 - Chicago - 1969

Thank You (Falettinme Be Mice Elf Agin) - Sly and The Family Stone - 1969

Use Me - Bill Withers - 1972

It's Your Thing - Isley Brothers - 1969

Standing on Shaky Ground - Temptations - 1975

Higher Ground - Stevie Wonder - 1973

Fopp - Ohio Flyers - 1975

Shining Star - Earth Wind and Fire - 1975

Red Clay - Freddy Hubbard, et.al. - 1970

Long Train Runnin - Doobie Brothers - 1973

Afternoon Delight - Starland Vocal Band - 1976

Cosmic Slop - Funkadelic - 1973

Ramblin Man - Allman Brothers Band - 1973

Long Haired Country Boy - Charlie Daniels - 1974

Devil Went Down to Georgia - Charlie Daniels - 1979

Book 3 Songs - Lincoln's Shame

Welcome To The Jungle - Guns N' Roses - 1987

Skin Tight - Ohio Players - 1974

We Only Just Begun - The Carpenters - 1970

Fly Like an Eagle - Steve Miller Band - 1976

Tiny Bubbles - Do Ho - 1966

That's Amore - Dean Martin - 1953

Magic Carpet Ride - Steppenwolf - 1968

I Shot The Sheriff - Bob Marley - 1973

Book 4 Songs - Lincoln's War

Love - George Duke - 1974

Creepin - Grand Funk Railroad - 1973

Uptown - Prince -1980

Reasons - Earth Wind & Fire - 1975

I'm Every Woman - Chaka Khan - 1978

Dreaming of You - Blackbyrds - 1977

Casey Jones - Grateful Dead - 1978

I Gotcha - Joe Tex -1972

Get Up Offa That Thing - James Brown -1976

All photos taken by Michael R. Pope

(Except this one)

Your adventure is my adventure,

Thank you

Book 3 - Lincoln's Shame
The Conspiracy Unravelling
1st Edition

Book 4 - Lincoln's War
The Fight For Life
Release 07/24

Links to Lincoln's Ghetto Series

AMAZON BOOKS
https://qrco.de/bebyUK

Barnes & Noble
https://qrco.de/becEj9

Connect with Michael R. Pope

Web Site
http://lincolnsghettoseries.com

Newsletter Info
https://qrco.de/bemKU3

IG - @mpopemedia
https://www.instagram.com/mpopemedia/

Facebook - Michael R. Pope
https://qrco.de/bemKPt

To learn more about Lincoln Illinois go to:

http://findinglincolnillinois.com/alincolnandpostville.html

Lincoln's Ghetto
The America
Many Call Home

MPM

MPope Media

Printed in Great Britain
by Amazon